BRAZILIAN'S NINE MONTHS' NOTICE

BY

SUSAN STEPHENS

MILLS BOON

First published in Great Britain 2015
By Mills & Boon, an imprint of HarperCollins*Publishers*
1 London Bridge Street, London, SE1 9GF

Large Print edition 2016

© 2015 Susan Stephens

ISBN: 978-0-263-26163-9

Printed and bound in Great Britain
by CPI Antony Rowe, Chippenham, Wiltshire

For my friend, the wonderfully warm
and talented Carole Mortimer,
in this, her very special year.

CHAPTER ONE

HAVING THE NIGHT off from her job as chambermaid to attend the wedding of her best friend in Scotland should have been a cause for celebration. A racing heart made that impossible, because Lucas Marcelos would almost certainly attend the wedding too, which meant no swerving from the truth.

Luc...

Would she ever learn?

No, Emma concluded, staring into the mirror in the ladies room at her rabbit-in-the-headlights face. Her stomach clenched at the thought of meeting up with the man who had fathered her unborn child. There was no doubt. She had taken a pregnancy test three times. It was only a couple of weeks since she'd left London and the bed of the hotel owner and infamous bad boy of gaucho polo, Lucas Marcelos—too early for doctors or scans, or even the physical signs to make themselves felt, other than tender breasts and some nausea, which, she had no doubt, would ramp up when she faced Luc.

The self-professed playboy was hardly going to leap with joy when he heard her news. He certainly wouldn't show the same warm charm he had in London. A man as wealthy and successful as Lucas was bound to be suspicious of her motives. He would be even more suspicious if he knew how elated she'd been when she had discovered she was pregnant.

Emma's main worry wasn't for herself. She wondered if Luc would make a good father for her baby. They hardly knew each other, and what she did know about him hardly pointed to him being a family man.

One step at a time, she told herself firmly, checking the dress that had seemed perfectly fine when she had first walked into the cloakroom and now seemed too tight. Luc was a close friend of the groom so he was bound to be here.

The groom, Tiago Santos, was marrying one of Emma's closest friends, Danny Cameron. When Luc could spare the time from his chain of super-luxury hotels, both men played gaucho polo for the world-famous Thunderbolt polo team. If Luc didn't show up he would be the only member of team Thunderbolt not attending the wedding. Emma had recognised several striking faces from the team's publicity photos. Odds on, Lucas was prowling the party right now.

She'd been on Luc's hotel training course in London when the principal of the college had brought her to his attention. Luc's menacing glamour had caused quite a stir at the annual prize-giving ceremony, where Emma had been singled out for special praise for having an extraordinary grasp of the hotel industry. Because she'd cared for his staff and had seen ways to streamline their jobs, Emma had insisted when Luc had praised her afterwards. 'You interest me,' he'd said, his dark eyes mesmerising. She just hadn't realised how much.

The instant that faintly amused stare had landed

on her awestruck face, she had been lost. She'd always been a romantic and Lucas Marcelos more than lived up to his formidable reputation. He *was* built like a gladiator, and he *did* look like a god of the underworld, as some of the more colourful media reports had commented. With his wavy black hair, swarthy complexion, sharp black stubble and hard, driven face, Lucas was a primal force, and his interest had led her to progress to a wholly unrealistic fantasy along the lines of working alongside him and seeing him every day.

When he had stayed on in London this had seemed almost possible, and she had worked hard to maintain a professional front and impress him. As the days had stretched into weeks, she had allowed herself to believe they could be friends. She had opened up to him about her hopes for her future and her dreams of a career within his company. She had been flattered by his continued interest, she supposed now—too naïve to realise that Luc was a practised seducer who could adapt his technique to suit the situation—or that, for a short time, she had been that situation and her chastity had been a challenge Luc had been determined to overcome.

It had all come to a head on the night she had learned that her parents had been killed in a police chase. She had been so devastated she hadn't told anyone. She certainly hadn't told Luc, as she would have had to explain her parents' criminal past and her own deep-seated grief, which she couldn't explain even to herself.

Her parents had never wanted her, and had always referred to her as their accidental child. That hadn't stopped her loving them, or pursuing an endless quest to win their love. She had made excuses to herself—her beautiful mother found ageing difficult to handle, while her father, a member of the aristocratic Fane family, must have found the pressure to succeed unbearable. On the night they'd died her tears had been genuine—sorrow for them and the lives they had wasted, and acceptance that her long-held dream to find a way to make them love her, had been lost. She could remember the overwhelming need to be held and loved overcoming her.

Pretend love was better than no love at all, and Luc was a master of seduction. She had been so glad of it that night. He had woken her to pleasure so extreme she'd found she could forget everything. And so the fantasy had progressed for one more night. Lucas Marcelos had then been her adoring lover, and she had been his treasured love. She had even asked him at one point where they would go from there. Luc had looked at her with surprise, and then he'd shrugged. 'We could have an affair, if you like.'

Her dreams had shattered. And then he'd laughed, as if such things were all too easily arranged. She had waited until he'd been asleep and had slipped out of his bed, making the long trek home to Scotland, thinking that would get her head straight. In going back home, she'd hoped to find some trace of a happy memory with her parents, but there had been no trace. There had been nothing to find. So she'd got a job here and started to rebuild her life. She had never thought to see Luc again, but now he was back in her life, for however short a time, she would have to tell him about the baby.

At least she was back in touch with reality now, Emma reflected as she smoothed the fine silk dress over her still-flat stomach. Lucas was a devastatingly handsome billionaire. She was a chambermaid in training. There was no common ground between them. And skulking in the ladies room wasn't the answer. She had to face him. With her life as it stood now, she couldn't afford to waste any more time on hopeless causes. She'd feel better when she explained how happy she was to be expecting a child, and that she didn't need his help, now or ever.

He probably wouldn't even remember her, Emma reflected as a crowd of women joined her in the cloakroom. As they jostled for space at the mirror she reached for her small pouch of cosmetics and set about improving the things she could. Too much make-up and she'd look as if she'd painted her courage on. Too little and Luc might think her pale and weak. And she would never allow him to think that. Adding some lip-gloss helped, and blusher worked wonders. She was just putting everything away again when one of the women turned to her. 'Hi. Great party, isn't it?'

'Have you seen who's here?' another woman chipped in.

'Lucas Marcelos!' a third exclaimed, faking a swoon as she directed a knowing look at her friends. 'I wonder if any of us will come to his attention tonight?'

Emma was glad of the raucous laughter as it gave her a chance to recover. 'He's here?' she confirmed once they had calmed down.

'And alone,' the first woman confided. Raising a brow, she added, 'Men like him shouldn't be allowed out without a leash. Have you seen him?' She fanned herself. 'He's a licence to sin. Who could blame us if we had to give him a test drive?'

Emma said nothing as the women continued to discuss their sighting of the notorious heartbreaker. Her first impulse was to run as far and as fast as she could. She was pregnant by a rich and powerful man—a man she hardly knew, with a reputation for ruthlessness and womanising. To top that off, she was penniless in a dead-end job. A job that would lead places, she was determined, calming herself down, and motherhood didn't come with a handbook, but, like countless women, she would do her best for her child with or without a man's help. She wasn't running anywhere. She would see this out. She had never been a quitter, except for that one night in London when she'd run from the most devastating man she had ever met, because she couldn't bear to be hurt again, but now there was a child to consider, and she would never run away again. Her child wasn't an accident, it was a gift.

Feeling better, she collected up her things. Danny had lent her a beautiful dress to wear, and both Danny and the chief bridesmaid, Lizzie, another of her childhood friends, would be waiting for her, wondering where she was. Smoothing down the dress, she checked her reflection in the mirror one last time. Pregnancy and Lucas was a dizzying combination, but the make-up had helped to conceal her ashen complexion. She just had to get through tonight. She had to find a way to talk to him that kept the facts central and emotion out of it.

She could do this. She turned to say good-night to the women. 'Have a great party—' And stepped out of the door, straight into the path of Lucas.

Her shocked gaze flashed to his face as he steadied her. Luc's touch was so familiar she felt faint for a moment. It was as if they had never been apart. His dark stare was just as penetrating, his firm mouth still as tempting. Her lips tingled with anticipation, even as her stomach clenched with alarm.

'Are you okay?'

His husky voice caressed her senses. It was the same voice that had lulled and thrilled her while he had directed her pleasure.

'Yes, I'm fine, thank you.' She pulled back to put some space between them. Theorising was all very well, but standing in front of Luc again had completely thrown her. 'Apologies for bumping into you,' she said lightly, relying on good manners to get her through a difficult situation.

'We know each other, don't we?'

He was teasing her. They definitely knew each other. Luc knew every inch of her body intimately. 'I believe we've met.' She cursed her body for its instant response when her aim was to act cool.

Luc's ebony brows swept up, making him look like a Tartar from the plains on a raid. Tall, dark and dangerous, with watchful eyes, he was exactly as she remembered him—except for the clothes. He'd been naked when she'd left him. The formal black tailoring suited him. White shirt, grey silk tie, black diamond cufflinks, accessorised with a killer smile, Lucas Marcelos was every bit the awe-inspiring billionaire, while she was every bit the chambermaid in her borrowed dress. She turned to go.

Luc stepped in front of her. His heat enveloped her. His potent sexuality threatened to seduce her all over again.

'I hope you enjoy your evening, Senhor Marcelos,' she said formally, looking past him towards the ballroom, where the party was in full swing.

'Why did you leave London so suddenly, Emma?'

Why didn't he get out of her way? 'It was time to go.' She kept her tone carefully neutral, wanting to put some distance between them so she could get her head together. This wasn't the time or place to tell him she was pregnant with his child, but the time would come and she wanted to be ready for it. She shrugged. 'I had places to be.' She met his stare levelly, hoping he would leave it there.

Luc didn't leave it.

'I thought you were happy in your job. I thought all my staff was happy?'

'I'm sure they are.'

'But you couldn't have been, or you wouldn't have left.'

Luc's stare had hardened. He expected her to answer, but her heart was beating so rapidly she doubted she could draw enough breath to speak.

'Did you find a better job?'

'Not really,' she admitted honestly, following Luc's stare around their surroundings. She got his message loud and clear. This hotel was lovely for a small town in the wilds of Scotland, but it was hardly on the scale of Luc's fabulous palaces. Maybe he thought their encounter in London had been a tactical move on her part to help her scramble up the career ladder faster, and when that hadn't worked out she'd come back here. Nothing could be further from the truth. She had worried their short-lived affair would compromise her career. Now she knew that sex was sex to Lucas, and had no bearing on his business. To her, sex was a promise and an endorsement of trust—she had thought. Thankfully, she knew better now.

'Did you return to Scotland for the wedding?' Luc enquired, staring at her intently.

'This is my home. I was born in Scotland. I work here. The bride was born here too, which is why Danny chose to get married at this hotel.'

'I heard your cousin Lizzie is the daughter of the local laird?'

'That's right.' She could practically hear the cogs whirring in his mind. If her cousin was the daughter of the local laird, why was Emma scrubbing floors?

Luc's frown deepened. 'So you have the same job here that you had in London?'

'Not quite. I'm still working as a chambermaid,' she confirmed proudly. Her uncle might be a laird, but Emma came from the poor branch of the Fane family, the notorious branch that had resorted to criminal activities rather than taking an honest job. That had never been her way, and, however meagre her wage packet, she had the satisfaction of knowing that she had earned every single penny herself. Circumstances at home might have resulted in her education being patchy, but she was changing that, studying at night, even though there was no hope of progression here. She still had ambitions for a career but had to keep working in the meantime, and now, with a child to consider, she had a real purpose and drive behind that ambition.

'Surely there's no possibility of advancement for you here?' Luc commented, as if he'd read her thoughts.

'No training programme either,' she confirmed, 'but it's a start.' She stared him down, as if daring him to contradict her. This wasn't her forever job. This was a job to help her get back on her feet. But it would seem odd to Lucas that she had come here to work in a hotel that couldn't offer its staff any of the advantages he could.

'You should have stayed in London.'

She recoiled at his tone. What business was it of his? Then she remembered the offer to become his short-term mistress. Did he think that had been a better prospect for her? If he did, he was alone.

That sensible determination wasn't enough to stop her mind taking off in one direction while her wilful body took off in another, and only one of those places was safe.

'You must be paid a lot less here than my company paid you in London.'

'Money isn't everything, Senhor Marcelos.'

'But it helps. And please call me Luc. I think both of us are grown-up enough to handle this situation, aren't we?' His steely stare homed in on her face.

Firming her jaw, she shrugged. 'I like it here. I'm happy here. I've got friends around me— friends who are waiting for me in the ballroom right now. So, if you will excuse me?'

Luc made her a mock bow. 'Forgive me for monopolising you. I will escort you back to your friends.'

Every second she spent with him was torture, because every second she spent with Luc was an opportunity to tell him about the baby, but could she really do that here, in a crowded hotel corridor?

'So, Emma, do you live here permanently now?'

'Not exactly here.' She glanced around. Luc's staff quarters were known to be some of the best in London, but though this hotel was comfortable in the public areas it was a lot less so in the parts the public never got to see. 'I really should be joining my friends.' She breathed a sigh of relief as Luc ushered her forward towards the dazzle and the noise of the party. They walked together, close but not touching—still close enough to make the women from the cloakroom gape and stare. If only they knew, they wouldn't be jealous, and she wouldn't be falling for Luc's brutal charm a second time. Satisfied she'd got everything in hand, she risked a smile as they parted.

'You look pleased with yourself,' he said.

And you're a practised seducer, she thought, her heart thumping wildly as she took in the suspicion in his face. 'I hope you enjoy the rest of your evening, Senhor Marcelos.'

'You too, Ms Fane.'

She would enjoy her evening. Lucas Marcelos would have to look elsewhere for his entertainment tonight.

CHAPTER TWO

HE WOULD HAVE known her anywhere. The bolt of lust he'd experienced in London was back. Emma Fane had invaded his senses again, making the ache in his groin a permanent fixture. Hearing her scream with pleasure in his arms seemed to have happened moments ago. He had wanted to lead her from the wedding reception, not towards it—find a quiet room where they could continue what they'd started—but for some reason he had sensed that she was holding him at bay.

His lips pressed down as he thought about it. He never bedded the staff. Emma had been an exception. Something about her had driven him to possess her, and as he entered the ballroom now, his hunting instinct sharpened as he spotted her right away. One taste of Emma Fane could never be enough for him.

'This is your table, sir,' the waiter said, distracting him.

He thanked the man, who had recognised him immediately. The seat was perfect. It gave him an excellent view of Emma. Seated between the bride and the chief bridesmaid, she appeared relaxed and animated, not a bit like the girl who had confronted him with such icy self-control outside the cloakroom. Of course she would have changed, he mused, trying to make sense of her manner. He'd learned only after she'd left his bed of the tragedy that would have brought her down to earth with a bump. Losing both her parents in a car chase with the police, only to discover they had been criminals on the run, would have been enough for anyone. The Fanes had been selfish and uncaring of their only child, by all accounts, but that didn't stop a person hunting for love, even if they knew their quest was hopeless.

When he'd first seen her, Emma had been full of fire, but she looked exhausted now. The job here, he reasoned as he studied her. She was more composed than she had been in London. An attractive air of maturity had settled over her, as if life had taught her some harsh lessons and she had come through. She'd been wild the night they'd wound up in his bed. Her zest for life had been contagious. Now he guessed her behaviour that night had been an attempt to blot out the pain, he suspected that Emma had used him in an attempt to forget.

That piqued his pride. It made him all the more determined to seduce her—to have her want him for more than forgetfulness. But why was she still here, working a job with no future? Surely she could have stayed in Scotland for the funeral and then returned to her job and the training course in London? Was she trying to avoid him? And, if so, why?

'Three beautiful women, aren't they?' the older woman sitting next to him commented.

He only realised now that he had been ignoring his dining companion and had been staring fixedly at Emma. There was only one beautiful woman in this room as far as he was concerned. 'All the women in Scotland are beautiful, from what I've seen.' he said, in an attempt to make amends for his lack of manners.

'And you are another charmer from Brazil,' the older woman observed shrewdly. 'But our women seem to like you dangerous men.'

He huffed a smile as he stared at the groom. Tiago Santos had been a notorious heartbreaker until the bride, Danny, had tamed him. The matron of honour, Lizzie, was married to another member of the Thunderbolt polo team, and Chico Fernandez had hardly been noted for his scrupulous behaviour when it came to women before he'd met his wife.

He had no intention of changing, Luc determined as he turned to make up for his poor manners at the dinner table. 'I trust you won't find me too threatening tonight?' he teased his wily companion.

'I shall keep you at arm's length,' she assured him with a twinkle in her eyes. 'Forty years ago it might have been a different story. Just don't hurt her,' the matriarch added, her face turning serious as she stared at him unblinking.

'Who are you taking about?' he said, frowning as if he didn't know what she meant.

'Emma Fane.' She gave him a look. 'It's no use trying to fool me, young man. I know exactly who you've been looking at. And my warning stands firm. That one's had more trouble in her life than she deserves.'

He knew better than to deny his interest in Emma. She was in his sights. Hearing the affection with which his neighbour had just described her made him all the more determined to hunt her down. Emma Fane intrigued him. She aroused him. He wouldn't let her get away from him a second time.

The band was playing. The ballroom was glittering with chandeliers, crystal and silver as it played host to an elegantly dressed crowd. But all Emma could see was Lucas. She pretended not to notice him. She had thought it would be easy to save all her attention for her friends, but couldn't stop her gaze wandering, and each time she looked at Luc he was looking back. She found that thrilling and dangerous, like a promise that this wasn't over yet. When the time came for her to leave her seat and help the bride get ready to leave the party with the groom, Luc was waiting for her in the hall.

She wasn't ready for this. She would never be ready for this.

'I'm sorry,' she said, adding a regretful smile, 'I really can't talk to you now.'

'When?' Luc demanded, his voice uncompromising.

'I'm busy. Can't you see?' She stared pointedly after the bridal party as they started up the stairs.

'Make time.'

'I beg your pardon.' She shot him a look.

'You heard what I said,' he repeated harshly.

'You make it sound irresistible,' she countered.

Luc glared at her. His voice held that same edge of command she remembered from London. It was the voice that had made her body thrill. Ignoring the pulse of lust, she moved past him.

He stopped her with his hand on her arm.

'Let me go.'

'No.'

His face was close, his eyes were blazing messages she didn't want to see. 'Are you always so direct?' She pulled away, tightening the tension between them.

'You should know,' he murmured drily.

Sensation rocked through her. She remembered every one of Luc's instructions. It didn't help that his wicked mouth was tugging in the faintest of smiles as he stared into her eyes. He was letting her know that he understood the effect he was having on her. 'I seem to remember you like me to be direct—and to direct you,' he said.

'How could you bring that up now?' Her voice was low and tense as she glanced around, wondering who might have heard him.

Luc shrugged.

'Excuse me, Senhor Marcelos. I need to go.'

'Luc,' he corrected her, his mouth tugging faintly.

Shaking her head with impatience, she tried

again to move past him, and hated herself for being disappointed when he moved away first, holding his hands up as if he couldn't wait to be rid of her. Was she so easily seduced by Luc's black charm?

No. She was not, Emma decided. Running up the magnificent staircase to catch up with the bride, she didn't give him a backward glance.

He showered at first light with the temperature turned to ice. Nothing helped. He huffed a smile at his physical reaction to thoughts of Ms Emma Fane. She was only a matter of yards away, which didn't help. She slept in the staff quarters beneath the eaves, the floor above his room, one of the housemaids had told him with a cheeky smile.

Securing a towel around his waist, he glanced at his face in the mirror and raked his hand through his hair. He couldn't get Emma out of his head. He had to do something about this. She had bewitched him in London and that memory hadn't died. Having slept on the problem, he thought he knew why she'd come home. Sometimes in life it was necessary to reboot before moving on, and where better could she do that than here amongst friends?

Towelling down roughly, he threw on his jeans, wondering where she was now. She had run away last night like Cinderella when the clock struck twelve—to look after the bride, she'd said. To avoid talking to him, he'd thought.

Maybe she had a boyfriend?

He swore viciously at the thought—then remembered he hadn't seen her with anyone at the party.

Maybe her boyfriend worked at the hotel and couldn't get away from his job?

Maybe. Emma Fane was an attractive woman. It seemed unlikely that she was on her own.

And who cared? It was none of his business. To hell with Emma Fane!

Glancing in the mirror, he parked the idea of a shave, but then he made the mistake of glancing at the bed and remembering their night in London. Having Emma in his bed had been one of the best parts of that night. She'd been wild for it, and he'd been only too happy to oblige. He tore his gaze away regretfully. He didn't have time for distractions like that. He wasn't just here for the wedding. He had a castle to buy, along with some other business to attend to. Neither was he an adolescent to waste his day fantasising about having sex with Emma Fane. Forget her. Breakfast, and then work…

Forget Emma?

Would she be working today?

Why not? She was a regular girl with a regular job.

Snatching up the phone, he called Housekeeping. 'I need some more towels in here, please.'

Emma was a regular girl?

He laughed at the thought. No way was Emma a regular girl. Nothing about her resembled the women he knew, from her generous figure to the way she took him on. None of the women he knew would dare to take him on. They wouldn't risk spoiling things. They expected him to lavish his time and money on them and then they repaid him in bed. Emma expected nothing from him.

In fact, the less she had to do with him, the better she seemed to like it, or so it appeared to him.

He paced the room, weighing up the odds of getting the result he wanted. Even a hotel this size must surely employ more than one chambermaid.

He didn't have to wait long to find out. There was a knock on the door, and a voice called out 'Housekeeping.'

Emma.

'Towels, sir? Oh, for goodness' sake!' Emma blurted before she could stop herself.

Luc laughed, his eyes black with hidden thoughts. 'You didn't think to check the name of the guest requesting towels?' he challenged as he admitted her into his room.

'I'm not expected to address the guests by name, sir.'

Luc's lips pressed down with disapproval as he observed tersely, 'Poor training.'

'Safer for the staff,' she countered, walking

past him. 'We're not encouraged to be familiar with the guests.'

'Even those you know, Emma?' Luc called after her.

Her spine tingled as his stare warmed her back. 'Even those I know,' she confirmed coolly.

She knew this man very well indeed, and not at all, Emma realised as she headed for his bathroom. There had been very little talking, other than about the running of the hotel, in London, and even less last night. For once in her life she'd managed to remain sensible, and had steered well clear of Lucas.

'Don't you have anything to say to me, Emma?' Luc's lips pressed down in mock affront when she emerged from the bathroom, having finished arranging his towels.

'Sorry, sir. That's not what I'm here for.' This was definitely not the moment to tell him about the baby. When she did that, she wanted it to be a private chat, but in a public place. Straightening her back, she made straight for the door. Luc opened it for her, and she avoided his gaze as she told him, 'If you want anything else just call Housekeeping and they'll send someone—'

'But maybe not you?' he interrupted.

'Maybe not me,' she agreed, turning to meet his stare head on. 'It all depends who's on duty.'

'When do you get off duty, Emma?'

Her heart thundered. 'Me?' She frowned. 'When my shift is over.' Slipping past him, she could only think of leaving his room and reaching the safety of the kitchens downstairs.

She had barely opened the door to the kitchen when the head of housekeeping turned her around. 'He's ringing again,' she said with a look. 'Apparently, he's run out of coffee now.'

But she'd filled up the tray when she'd serviced Luc's room. What could he want now? Biting back her anxious thoughts, she made sure the service trolley had everything she required, and was back outside Luc's room within five minutes of leaving it. 'Yes, sir?' she said politely as he opened the door. 'Here I am with everything you could possibly need.' She couldn't help herself. She was fuming.

'If only,' he murmured, and she suspected he was trying not to laugh.

She pushed her trolley past him, wondering if the moment would ever come when she could tell him about the baby. Was now the time to tell him? Should she close the door and beard the lion in his den?

Could she afford to lose this job?

No. And he might just erupt in fury—ring downstairs and get her sacked. Propositioning a guest? That was a sackable offence. Threatening him? Goodness knew, she couldn't risk that appearing on her CV.

'Problem?' he queried, no doubt wondering at her silence.

Calming herself, she took stock. He was just a man—a formidable man, but a living, breathing human being just as she was. She would speak to him when the time was right. There was no need to feel panicked into it.

'Lovely day,' he commented, turning to look out of the window.

She couldn't tell if he was joking or not. The

snow was drifting down, and it was a chocolate-box scene outside, but frigidly cold, while Luc was the polar opposite. He looked so hot dressed just in jeans and a casual shirt. He looked hot in everything—

Especially naked.

'My apologies for not noticing that you had run out of coffee,' she said, trying to remain cool and professional. 'I should have noticed when I brought up the towels.'

'No problem.' He turned and seemed to look at her a little longer. 'I only just noticed the lack of it, or I wouldn't have called you back.'

She doubted that somehow, but gave him one of the thin smiles she reserved for those times when guests were difficult and pride in her job wasn't enough.

'When does your shift end today?' he asked, catching her off guard as she organised his fresh supplies.

Was he suggesting they get together when her shift ended? It would give her chance to talk about the baby... But his voice was too intimate, too darkly amused. Luc wasn't going to suggest a quiet talk over a cup of coffee, she suspected.

'I'm not sure,' she said on a dry throat. 'That all depends.' She hurried to move the trolley towards the door. Luc was leaning against the wall, watching her like a tiger with a mouse.

'That's all right, you can go now,' he said, opening the door for her.

She breathed a sigh of relief to be let off the hook. She'd choose the time, and she would choose the place to tell him.

'See you later,' he said.

His warm, clean scent washed over her as she moved past him. Luc had recently showered, and his hair was still damp. Waving in disarray, it had caught on his stubble. He hadn't shaved.

And why should she care? Emma decided as she pushed her trolley out into the corridor.

Fit, tall and hard, wearing snug-fitting jeans, Lucas Marcelos was a formidable sight. She cared. 'Will there be anything else, sir?' she enquired in her best professional voice. But then some demon must have climbed inside her throat.

'Perhaps you'd like your shoes cleaned or your trousers pressed?' *With you still wearing them, preferably,* her hostile face clearly said. 'How about the bed? Would you like me to straighten that before I leave?'

That was absolutely the wrong thing to say, she realised as a slow smile curved his mouth. Luc really knew how to use a bed. And not just to lie in it.

'Why don't you come back later to do that? I'll put a sign outside my door when I'm ready for you.'

With difficulty, she curbed her thoughts and managed to say nothing in reply, other than a polite 'Yes, sir.'

'There is one thing.'

'Yes, sir?' she repeated with studied patience.

'Tell Housekeeping they need to get bigger towels.'

None of their guests was half his size. Luc was a towering presence in every way. 'Will there be anything else, sir?'

'Yeah. How long do you plan to keep this up?'

'Keep what up, sir?' She waited a moment. 'If there's nothing else, sir?'

'Not for now.'

He leaned back against the door and laughed. On each meeting he liked Emma more. It wasn't just her voluptuous form, her flame-red hair or her spiky nature—though he liked that a lot. She might look young and vulnerable with that pale Celtic beauty, but beneath her demure uniform-clad exterior Emma Fane was still the firebrand he remembered and had enjoyed. She was everything he'd craved when he'd first seen her in London, and he was in no way done with her yet.

She'd improved, he concluded as he pulled a sweater over his shirt. She was more assured. While in London he hadn't been very interested in her personality, he had detected that she was bolder now, though she'd been bold enough then—a wild thing, furious with passion. She was different now. Steely.

It was only natural she would have toughened up after her parents' accident and the subsequent brutal press revelations. He was impressed with her control, and the polite words she'd trotted out, delivered with that fiery emerald stare. That wasn't something he was going to forget in a hurry.

Picking up the keys to his car, he looked around and thought the room seemed empty without her. Emma was a small woman with plenty of character. She'd been too busy with her bridesmaid's duties for them to get together last night, and then she had taunted him with the lilting laugh she reserved for her friends. Her reddened, careworn hands hadn't changed, he mused as he left the room and strolled down the corridor towards the bank of elevators. He had noticed them in London, with particular reference to the magic such work-worn hands could weave—once she had been shown how to use them and had been encouraged.

Nodding politely to his fellow guests, he entered the elevator still thinking about Emma. When she had disappeared out of his bed in London in the middle of the night, his enquiries had proved he wasn't the only one to be surprised by her disappearance. Emma was such a good worker, he'd been told, and had such great prospects of advancement in the business. Well, he'd noticed that in her himself. Why would she leave? Where would she go? She was renowned for putting in long hours without complaint, and always making the best of every situation. What had happened to Emma Fane had been the question on everyone's lips. He knew now that she was making the best of a bad situation. But did he know anything about that situation?

Emma Fane was trouble he didn't need, he told himself firmly as he stood back to let the other guests spill out into the lobby first. He admired her professionalism, but it riled him that she could treat him like any other guest. After their night in London he'd expected more.

Giving him the chance to turn her down?

Okay. Yes. His pride was bruised. He had never been wrong-footed by a woman before. Had Emma forgotten that he'd made her scream with pleasure in his arms? Or was that why she was keeping her distance from him? Couldn't she trust herself around him?

He liked that version best, and smiled as he waited for the valet to bring his car round. There was no basis for his obsession with Emma. Full lips, full breasts and shapely legs—all great, but he wasn't about to fall at the feet of a flame-haired temptress simply because she was dressed in a severely cut uniform that demanded it be ripped off her. Tipping the valet, he got into his car.

All that day he lectured himself on steering clear of a woman who affected him so badly he couldn't concentrate. Hadn't he vowed never to become plagued by a woman again? He'd kept that pledge up to now—apart from that one slip in London with Emma. When he'd woken that morning he'd been almost glad she'd gone— until he'd started missing her. Hadn't he learned that caring destroyed lives, or that hunger for a woman could so easily become an obsession? He wasn't going down that blind alley ever again.

So why was he still thinking about Emma Fane?

Because she was making herself unavailable to him, and that was a situation he would not allow to continue.

With the last appointment of the day done and dusted, he gunned the engine and released the handbrake. Thanks to Emma, he was aching with frustration. If he couldn't get her out of his head he would continue to be distracted. And that wasn't going to happen. He had to do something about Emma Fane. And soon.

CHAPTER THREE

LUC MARCELOS. SEX GOD. Damaged hero, according to the press, though whatever that meant had been carefully hushed up, Emma reflected as she hurried about her final tasks of the day.

That was another advantage of being as rich as Croesus. If people wanted to feed at his trough, they had to kowtow to Senhor Marcelos. Yes, there'd been talk about his past—nothing specific, a few high-profile affairs and some mammoth business deals. He let certain gossip get through on purpose, she suspected, so that the things he really cared about remained hidden. She could see something swirling behind his eyes and knew she wasn't imagining it, because she had the same hurt and shadows in her own stare. They were both private people who relied on themselves and no one else, but she couldn't pretend that Luc's shadows didn't intrigue her, or that she wouldn't like to know more about him, what made him tick.

Must she always go looking for trouble?

Apparently, yes, or she would have found some excuse not to service his room. One of the other chambermaids at the hotel would have jumped at the chance to take over from her.

Why didn't she ask them?

Not a chance.

It didn't matter how dangerous Luc might be— while he was here she couldn't stay away from him. There was a good reason for that. She had to find the right moment to tell him about the baby, and at some point he would leave Scotland for destinations unknown. Luc had homes all over the world, and could go to any one of them. Before he left she had to talk to him. He was hardly going to leave her a forwarding address.

When her shift was over she ran up the back stairs to her room. Her thoughts were still just as confused. Her main aim was to be a good parent, and to be as honest as she always had been, which meant coming clean with Luc, but each time she saw him her head reeled and her thoughts scrambled. How was she supposed to form a sound judgement about a man she only knew by reputation?

It didn't help that Luc seemed to think she was still that girl he knew from London, the girl who would go to bed with him at the drop of a hat. He couldn't know that things had changed radically for her since then. She'd been half-crazy with grief and shock that night and in her furious despair had found release and pleasure with him, but her reality had changed and she had no excuse now.

Safe in her tiny box room beneath the eaves, she lay on her narrow cot and thought about Luc... Luc naked. Luc looming over her, bronzed and immense, his wild black hair waving around his face, his stubble thick, his mouth firm and curving in a wicked invitation to sin. He hadn't needed to seduce her. She had been seduced at her first sight of him. He had made her body sing. He had inhabited every part of her, mind, body and soul, and with pleasure had come oblivion, which was all she'd craved.

So she had no excuse for still wanting him. She was back on her feet now and had more sense. She should steer clear—except she couldn't, because there was a baby to consider now. Sinking down onto the edge of the bed, she frowned, trying to imagine a situation where they could face each other and talk sensibly. It didn't seem likely they ever would. Luc had never been interested in conversation. She had to change that.

How?

Luc had a world of women at his beck and call. How was she going to persuade him that becoming a father would be so much more rewarding?

She shivered as memories of her own father came flooding back. He hadn't wanted her. He hadn't changed his life for her. However hard she had tried to win his love, he had rejected her. Was that what she wanted for her child?

She had to clear her mind and stop panicking. It was better that her child knew its father, rather than that it grew up searching and hoping and hunting for some elusive role model that didn't exist. And she had a nest egg to build up fast. She couldn't afford to lose this job. She had to provide a good home for her child. That was more important than anything else.

Examining her reflection in the mirror, she straightened her uniform and smoothed her hair. She took pride in what she did, and that wasn't going to change, but she had to face facts. Lucas Marcelos was fabulously wealthy with an aristocratic lineage stretching back to antiquity. She was the last in a long line of black sheep. How likely was it that Luc would take her seriously when she told him about their child? He was more likely to think she was trying to scam him and get money out of him with the news that she was pregnant. But she knew the truth and could hold her head up high. And she wasn't the first of her friends to deal with a bad boy.

The next morning, she straightened her room with new purpose before going downstairs to start work. She had decided to tell Luc today how things stood. Only then could she get on with her life. He was going back to Brazil, so they would both get a chance to think things through quietly before they came to any decision about the future. Telling him shouldn't be so hard. The entire Thunderbolt team was composed of bad boys, and her friends Lizzie and Danny had married two of them...

Why would that make it easier for her? She had no interest in taming Luc.

No. She had better things to do. Like working hard and raising a child. She certainly didn't have any more time to waste daydreaming.

The first bombshell to hit her when she arrived in the staffroom was the news that Lucas Marcelos wasn't leaving until the end of the week. All her thoughts of telling him and then them both having chance to think things through calmly while they were half a world apart crashed and burned. Luc would be right here. The consequences of telling him would be in her face.

'And he's calling for more towels,' the housekeeper announced, draining the remaining blood from Emma's face. 'The new big ones I bought especially for him.'

'More towels?' one of the chambermaids queried with a frown. 'I just took him some more towels.'

'It's not for us to question our guests,' the housekeeper reprimanded as she continued with her work.

Luc would keep on calling for one thing or another until she went upstairs to see him, Emma guessed. 'Don't worry, I'll go,' she said, wanting to make an end of it. It was better to face him now than allow this charade to continue.

He looked up at the knock on the door. 'Come in.' Putting his newspaper down, he stood up then relaxed as Emma used her pass card to open the door.

'Towels,' she told him briskly, sidestepping him as she walked into the room.

'Coffee?' he suggested, watching her back view appreciatively as she disappeared into the bathroom.

'Do you need more coffee?' she asked him with a touch of impatience.

'I have all the coffee I need, thank you. I just thought you might like a cup.'

'I'm afraid that wouldn't go down very well with my boss.'

'You never used to worry about what your boss thought.'

She chose not to answer him. He moved in front of her so she couldn't leave. 'You've still got a job in London, if you want it.'

'As what? Your part-time mistress?' she said in the same clipped and professional voice.

Nothing quite so permanent, he thought as his appetite sharpened. 'You could continue your training course.'

'Thanks for the offer.'

'And?' he prompted.

'And nothing.'

The lift of her brow said Emma believed he belonged to that group of gilded individuals who only had to look a certain way for a woman to fall at their feet. And she wasn't one of them.

She had carefully turned her face away from his naked chest. He hadn't thought about it until now. He had slipped on a shirt and jeans for the sake of decency after his shower, not wanting to slob around in a robe, and only noticed now that the shirt wasn't fastened.

'Luc, I need to talk to you—'

'And I to you,' he assured her, but they were interrupted by a second knock on the door. 'Breakfast. Hot coffee, freshly baked rolls. How can you resist?'

Easily, her look told him. Emma could resist the coffee and him.

She stood aside as he opened the door to let the waiter in, giving him all the chance he needed to admire her resolute profile: the firm mouth he loved to kiss, and the neat nose that made him smile when it wrinkled. Her expression right now was fixed in disapproval. How he'd love to soften that. He cleared the table for the waiter instead.

'Join me?'

'I beg your pardon?' she said.

He loved the way she drew herself up. She still

had to tilt her chin at an acute angle in order to meet his stare. 'Join me for breakfast—coffee at least,' he pressed as the waiter set out breakfast on his dining table.

'Sorry, sir. I can't do that,' Emma told him firmly.

He could just imagine the rumours flying around the kitchen after this. He should be more considerate and think about her reputation, but this was the woman who had clung to him and wrapped her naked limbs around him as she'd begged him for more. Why was she acting so cool now? He stopped her at the door with a hand on her shoulder, and turning his back on the waiter he murmured, 'Why don't you lighten up?'

'I'm not expected to lighten up,' she replied, matching his discretion. 'This is my job. I'm working.'

'So being pleasant to guests isn't part of your job description?'

'There are limits,' she said, glancing over his shoulder at the waiter.

'If you didn't work here, would you join me for coffee?'

'If I didn't work here, I wouldn't be in your room.'

She turned and seized hold of the doorhandle— so tightly her knuckles turned white. 'If you will excuse me?'

'Allow me,' he said.

There was a rapid transfer of hands as Emma whipped hers away before he could touch her. The waiter was ready to leave, and they both stood back to let him go. He tipped the man a fistful of coins. Once he was out of earshot he turned back to Emma. 'Are you sure you won't join me?'

'Completely sure,' she said firmly. 'May I go now, sir?'

There were dozens of things rampaging behind her eyes that he guessed she would like to say, but not now. He decided to push a little harder to find out what was on her mind. 'You do know I'm staying on for another few days?'

'Yes, I heard.'

She had turned back to face him, and again that unsaid something flashed across her face. 'If there's something you need to say to me, Emma, just spit it out.'

She looked genuinely shocked for a moment, and then reverted to her role of efficient hotel employee. 'Just call downstairs when you're ready to leave, and they'll have someone come up to collect your luggage.'

'I think I can manage the cases myself,' he gritted out. Digging into the back pocket of his jeans, he said, 'Here...for you.'

'What's this?' She frowned as he held out a twenty.

His patience was exhausted. 'It's money, Emma. What does it look like? It's common practice in the hotel industry to offer money for good service. I've had you running up and down for the past couple of days. A tip is customary in Scotland as well as in London, I presume?'

She flinched as he pressed the note into her hand. And then, very slowly and deliberately, she folded it and placed it on the table just inside his door. 'There are some excellent charities you can give this money to. But I'm not one of them. Have a good day, Senhor Marcelos,' she added with a cool stare. 'I hope you enjoy the rest of your stay.'

She'd changed—too much for him not to be suspicious. He watched with mixed emotions as Emma walked off down the corridor. From wild party girl to considered and efficient chambermaid, who looked as if butter wouldn't melt in her mouth, was quite a leap. And he didn't believe it for a minute. Pheromones were still dancing in the air. Round one to Emma, but the battle wasn't over yet. In London she'd been all fire and passion, but now she was thoughtful and distant. She must know she couldn't have prevented her parents' death, so what was eating her?

He didn't have time to waste thinking about it. He had business meetings stacked up end on end.

Emma remained in his head for the rest of the day—to the point where he cut things short, something he'd never done before, and all because he couldn't wait to get back to the hotel to see Emma.

When he arrived and saw her waiting for the elevator as he walked into the lobby, his hunting instincts sharpened. She sensed, rather than saw him, and turned around as he walked towards her. 'Good evening, Senhor Marcelos. I hope you've had a nice day?'

'A highly successful day, thank you.'

She gave him a look as if to say, *Is there any other kind of day for you?* She was dressed in her chambermaid's outfit with a kettle in her hand and more towels for another guest. The sight irritated him. They worked her to death here, and he hated the idea of Emma Fane waiting on anyone but him. She'd had such good prospects in London, which she had rejected, thrown away.

Why?

Once they were inside the elevator she didn't look at him but stared fixedly at the illuminated floor numbers above the door panel as they flashed on and off. Her wildflower scent filled his senses. She was soft and warm. He was big and hard. He radiated cold from the frigid temperature outside, while to his tortured imagination Emma appeared to be surrounded by a cosy if impenetrable glow. She was so tiny compared to him, yet they had fitted together so well, he remembered. His body remembered everything about her—everything that had happened that night. It made her coolness now all the more insulting.

The lift emptied and they were on their own for the last few floors.

'Come back to London with me, Emma,' he said as the lift slowed.

She turned to look at him with surprise and raised a brow.

'Don't allow the tragedy to destroy your life.'

'Thank you, but I'm quite capable of handling my own affairs, and I really don't want to talk about them with you.'

'Don't you?'

Her cheeks flamed red as if she was hiding something from him. He wondered what as she

went back to studying floor numbers as they
flashed on and off.

'I understand why you came home to Scotland,
but not why you stay here. It makes more sense to
go back to London and complete your training.'

'To you, maybe.'

His senses surged as she fired back at him. He
liked her like this, full of passion, full of fire.
'You can pick up the programme,' he insisted,
determined to keep the pressure on. 'Everyone
will understand that you needed time to come to
terms with what happened. It's a good course,
Emma—the best. And free to all my staff.'

'I know that,' she said, refusing to look at him.

'You had career prospects—great prospects.
Why are you throwing them away?'

'I'm happy here.'

The elevator slowed and the doors slid open,
but before she could walk through them he stood
in front of her. 'What do you get here that you
can't get in London? The chance to grow old and
grey while you wait for promotion?'

'Peace of mind,' she fired back, her eyes full of steel as she stared at him.

'So it's all about me?'

'Hah!' She laughed.

'Well, I can tell you what it's about here,' he drove on. 'It's all about dead men's shoes, while I have hotels around the world full of opportunity. You could work in any one of them—'

'You're pitching hard,' she interrupted. 'Why, Lucas?'

'What's your problem? I know there's something. Debts? A persistent boyfriend you can't get rid of? I don't know—'

'Don't you, Lucas?'

'There is something troubling you,' he said. 'If you had problems in London you should have told me.'

'Problems apart from you?' Her eyes were firing bullets at him. 'I didn't have any problems in London,' she assured him tensely.

'What, then?'

'Why can't you let it go? This isn't the time. I have work to do.'

'When will it be the time?'

She looked as if she would like to say something, but then thought better of it, and so he quietened his tone and said, 'If you have a problem, who else is going to help you?'

'You're going to help me?' Her mouth slanted sceptically.

'You trusted me in London. Why not now?'

'I trusted you,' she said, neither a question nor a statement. 'But you flew out of the country that morning. "Billionaire off on his travels again",' she quoted from the newspapers. 'Whether I'd left you or not, don't even pretend you were planning to stick around.'

'Did you expect me to stay and start something with you?'

'A proper relationship, do you mean?' She shook her head as if that had never entered her thoughts, and he believed her. 'I want to get out of the lift, if you don't mind,' she said, looking past him.

He moved aside. 'Think about what I've said,

Emma. There's still a place for you in London, if you want it.'

'I've just taken on more hours here,' she said, as if that was an end of the subject.

'We can still discuss it.'

'I've got a twelve-hour shift ahead of me.'

'Twelve hours?' He was aghast. 'How many hours have you put in so far today? There are laws to protect workers like you, Emma. This isn't the Dark Ages. Your hours would be capped at my hotel in London, and you'd still receive a decent wage.' She couldn't deny that he cared for his staff. 'My staff mean everything to me. Without them, I have nothing. They should treat you the same way here. Don't they ever give you time off?'

'I choose my hours, and I get enough time,' she assured him.

He exhaled, both with anger and frustration, as Emma slipped past him and walked away.

The last thing she heard as the steel door slid to was Luc's angry huff, but she had always worked hard. Growing up, there had only been one way to have new clothes and enough food on the table, and that had been to make the money herself. Whether her parents had made much out of their life of crime was hard to say. The only times she'd ever seen them they were so drunk or so high it would have the easiest thing in the world to steal from them, and they had died penniless and in debt, which she was also struggling to pay.

After she'd restocked the room, she headed up the stairwell, through the fire door onto the small balcony at the top of the fire escape. The air was so cold here it was like breathing in ice shards, but she needed to refresh herself and wake up in readiness for the next shift. She was exhausted with the pregnancy and exhausted from working double shifts, but she had to go on. She had to support herself and a child.

As a lone bird flew across her field of vision to its roost, she wished briefly that she could fly away. Lucas had used her for sex and moved on. She had used him for sex and moved on, so they were quits. If only she could forget about him once she had told him about their baby, but their child bound them together for life.

Hugging her stomach protectively, she started to agonise over how and when to tell him. The future of an unborn child was at stake, and she couldn't afford to get the timing wrong, and didn't want to think how Luc would take the news.

She worked harder than she ever had during the night shift in a failed attempt to put Lucas Marcelos out of her mind. Only one thing mattered, she kept telling herself fiercely, and that was her baby, and by the end of this shift she could add to her nest egg.

Though she scrubbed and cleaned and polished throughout the long night, Luc never left her mind. His baby was with her too. That was the one thought that kept her going, kept her happy, kept her calm. In spite of all the obstacles, she was so happy to be pregnant. From the first moment she'd suspected, the world had seemed a brighter place and she had vowed there and then that, whatever problems lay ahead of her, she would make a very different life for her child from the life she had known growing up.

Luc might have no part in raising their child. She had already accepted that and intended to ask nothing of him. She didn't need his help. She could do everything by herself, she always had. Telling him was the only difficult part, and that had seemed so easy in theory, but when she'd seen him face-to-face she'd known that nothing about it would be easy, and had panicked at the thought of him taking her baby away from her. Luc had the power to do that. He had the money and the influence she lacked. How would she even find her child if he decided to steal it away from her, when he had homes all over the world?

She had to lift her head from her scrubbing to take some deep, calming breaths. Becoming a shivering wreck wouldn't help her child.

Would a man like Luc turn his back when she told him? Would he allow her to carry on and remain in Scotland? No. He would interfere. But she still had to tell him. It was the right thing to do. But Luc would want his child to have a very different life from anything she could provide. His child would have a privileged life, with nannies and carers and expensive schools...

But no mother on hand.

No encumbrance of any kind would be allowed to interfere in the self-indulgent lifestyle of the infamous Lucas Marcelos. His child would reflect his wealth and status, while its mother could only be an embarrassment to him.

And now her throat felt as dry as tinder, and she remained cold and shivery for the rest of her shift. It was still dark when she finished work. The winter nights were long and cold this far north, and she had never felt so alone and uncertain as she put her cleaning equipment away and prepared to face the new day.

There were hormones racing through her system, she reminded herself, and these, coupled with simple exhaustion, meant she must pull herself together, and quickly. She had to carry on. She had a baby to think about now. Which meant keeping up her strength by eating something now.

Washing her hands and straightening her hair as best she could, she headed downstairs to the basement where the kitchen was located. There was always something good to eat. But not this morning, she discovered to her disappointment, because a hiking party had arrived unexpectedly, and paying guests always took precedence over staff.

'You'll have to go out for breakfast,' the chef told her with an apologetic shrug. 'I'm sorry, Emma. That's how it goes sometimes.'

'No problem.' She found a smile. 'You've got enough to do. I'll go into town and get something there.'

She was rocking on her feet for want of sleep, but she could buy something in town and bring it back to eat in her room. She didn't really care. She was too tired to think. Plucking her coat from the hook, she shrugged it on, and opening the back door she stepped outside from steaming warmth into the shock of the freezing air. Tucking her chin down, she was on the point of braving the walk into town when she stopped dead.

Dressed to brave the worst of a Scottish winter, Luc was leaning against the side of a sleek black sports car. 'How...?'

'I made enquiries to find out when your shift ended,' he said with a shrug. 'Are you satisfied now that you've completely exhausted yourself?'

'I'm fine.'

'You're not fine, Emma.' Opening the passenger door, he stood waiting for her to get in.

'What?' She couldn't even form the words. She was too tired to think.

Luc shook his head. 'We both know that what you're doing is against all regulations. The hotel could be fined for abusing its staff with these overly long hours, and then you really will be out of a job. Working through the night?' he said, his frown deepening. 'What are you trying to prove, Emma?'

'I'm not trying to prove anything,' she insisted.

Powerful arms folded across his rugged jacket, Luc disagreed. 'You'd better get in,' he said, 'before you freeze to death.'

And still she hesitated. 'I don't understand.'

'What's to understand, Emma?'

'Why are you waiting for me? I don't need a lift. I can walk into town.'

'Get in,' Luc repeated. 'I won't tell you again.'

CHAPTER FOUR

HE WASN'T JOKING. He practically lifted her into the car. She was glad of it. The pavements were icy—another thing the hotel had let slip. All the other parts of the pavement had been salted, but not here—they were treacherous, for guests, and for old folk in particular.

And for pregnant women, Emma reminded herself as Lucas settled her in the car. He even fastened the seat belt for her before closing the door, as if he knew how cold she was, and how exhausted. Walking around the sleek black vehicle, he got in and made himself comfortable on cream kidskin. She wasn't so tired she didn't notice that in jeans and rugged boots, with a jacket that emphasised the width of his shoulders, Luc looked like the perfect port in a storm.

At least this particular storm, Emma amended

as she gazed up into the snow-dappled air. She hadn't realised how cold she had become until now, when she was safely enclosed in the warm interior of Luc's luxury vehicle—every part of which called for wool or cashmere or alpaca, rather than a cheap nylon uniform beneath a thin, shabby coat. 'You don't have to do this,' she protested, suddenly self-conscious. She was having second thoughts as he pulled away from the kerb, thinking the type of place Luc would take her to for breakfast could only make her feel worse.

'You're going to eat and so am I,' he said. 'It would be churlish of me not to offer you a lift. I didn't fancy eating in a packed dining room or in my suite today.' He shrugged as he turned on the engine and moved into the stream of traffic heading into town. 'And you look as if you need a lift,' he added glancing at her.

'Thanks,' she said drily.

'I'm going to buy you breakfast. Get used to it, Emma.'

'I can buy my own breakfast.'

With a groan, he heaved a sigh. 'Emma,

please… Allow me to do this one small thing for you.'

'But you don't need to.'

'I know that, but I want to.' Luc flashed a glance at her. 'If you're still embarrassed about what happened in London, please don't be. This is just breakfast with a friend. Okay?'

If only.

'I'm not embarrassed,' she said, attempting a casual shrug.

'So relax.'

Luc turned on some music—easy listening, soothing and low, but still she couldn't relax as she tried to work out if there was enough time to tell him before they arrived in town. The longer she left it the harder it would be, but she'd had this dream that when she did tell him, they'd be relaxed with all the time in the world to talk things over. And, more importantly, she'd be on top form, with every argument for keeping the baby with her at her fingertips. Telling him now, when she was so tired, was a recipe for disaster.

'Stop,' he said, when she raked her hair with

her fingers, trying to improve her bedraggled appearance. 'You look great.'

'What? Like this?' From somewhere she found a laugh. 'I need a bath. I need to sleep. I need a miracle,' she finished wryly.

Luc glanced at her. 'At least you've got enough energy to smile.'

'Just,' she admitted ruefully.

'You'll feel better once you've had something to eat.'

She made no comment.

'What do you fancy?'

'I was just going to buy some food and take it back to my room. I'll embarrass you looking like this.'

'*Deus*, Emma. You're not the only person who works for a living. What do you have to be embarrassed about?'

She had no answer for him. This was a new side to Luc, and one she found hard not to like, but they had never really talked before, she realised. She really was a hopeless case. She didn't even know the man who was the father of her child. She didn't know where he stood about any-thing, beyond being considerate towards his staff. Luc didn't know her either. As her ex-employer, he knew the bones of her life story and no more. She was no stranger to Luc's efficient business manner, and as a woman in his bed she'd heard him swear and coax and laugh, but nothing more than that.

'Are you warm enough?' he asked when she shivered.

He didn't wait for her to answer. He just turned the heating up. If he hadn't been sitting next to her, she might have pinched some colour into her cheeks—or, better still, slapped them to wake up to the danger she was courting. How long was she going to wait before she told him? Should she do it now in the car—or in a café over a cup of tea? She had no time to think about this as Luc was already parking.

'We can walk from here,' he said.

Coming round to the passenger door, he insisted on helping her out. This new considerate Luc was a revelation, and she liked him. Too much.

The pavements had been gritted, and they were able to walk down the High Street at a brisk pace, past the familiar boutiques full of Scottish wares and trinkets. She flashed glances through the windows as she passed, as if to reassure herself that this was safe, this was home, and that nothing bad could ever happen here.

But it had. The car crash that had killed her parents had happened not a mile away—

'This okay for you?'

Luc had stopped outside the steamed-up windows of a café, she realised, quickly gathering her shattered senses. 'This is ideal.' It was. By some fluke, Luc had stopped outside her favourite café. He held the door for her, and the heat and appetising smells of home cooking instantly surrounded her, luring her in. She was surprised by his choice, but glad of it. It was a straightforward, no-frills café, where she wouldn't feel awkward dressed as she was, and where the food was all freshly prepared from local produce and delicious.

Needless to say, Luc created a wave of interest

from the moment he walked in. Even casually dressed, he stood out. No one had expected to have their breakfast interrupted by such a striking-looking man. Tall, hard-muscled, and tanned, he looked like an inhabitant from another planet where the sun shone more than once a year, and all the men were titans. Then the customers noticed Emma, which provoked an even bigger rustle of interest.

'What are you smiling at?' Luc demanded as they sat down.

'You chatting to people,' she remarked, having been surprised that Luc had exchanged greetings with quite a few people she knew.

'I've been in town awhile, and I have business here.'

And she'd seen this side of him at work, Emma remembered. Luc was naturally interested in people, which explained why he was so successful in the hospitality industry. But there was something else about his choice of café that surprised her too. 'You seem so at home, sitting on a plastic chair at a Formica-topped table,' she said wryly. 'Are you sure this isn't just to indulge me?'

'The food's the best here—I've tried it before. And I'm a human being just like you. I'm not some distant potentate, living in an ivory tower.'

No. Luc had a selection of ivory, she thought as he held up his hands in mock surrender.

'Do you always order for your guests?' she asked, after he'd ordered them both breakfast.

'When they look as tired as you do? Yes, I do. Don't fight it, Emma. Save your powder for the important battles ahead of you.'

She shrank inside at his words. It was as if he knew.

'This is only breakfast,' Luc was pointing out. 'If you want to change anything I've ordered, just ask the waitress. Or I will.'

'No. What you've ordered is fine. Thank you.'

'But next time ask me?' he suggested with an amused look. 'So…' He sat back. 'What shall we talk about while we wait for our breakfast to arrive?'

Her cheeks went fiery red. Short of hanging a notice around her neck plastered with the word 'baby', she couldn't think how she could look guiltier than she felt.

'Will you start or will I?' Luc prompted.

Making his big frame comfortable, he looked like a man at ease with himself and the world. She couldn't tell him. Not here. Too many people were listening. She had caused quite the stir coming in here with Lucas, where everyone knew her. She had lived in the village all her life, apart from when she'd gone down to London, and it was common knowledge that two of her friends, both local women, had married Brazilian men. People must be wondering if this was the latest romance. They also knew everything about her past.

Burying her face in the mug of tea the waitress had just brought them, she had to remember that however easygoing Luc might appear to be now, he would crack down the minute he heard about the baby. If she knew one thing about him, it was that Luc was all about control. Once he knew, everything would change and she wouldn't have a say in anything. She had to get things set up right from the start, which was much easier to plan than to do. Careless words now definitely wouldn't help her.

'Don't look so worried.' Leaning across the table, Luc stared her in the eyes. 'I don't expect you to divulge state secrets. I was just thinking what a good opportunity it was to release some tension and have a chat. You can start with the weather, if you like.'

She knew he was joking, but at least he'd made it possible to relax. She stared out of the window. 'If we were in Brazil, maybe the weather might be a topic we could talk about, but the less said here, the better, I think, don't you?'

She flinched as Luc's knee brushed hers. She was so on edge he had to notice. Guilt must be emblazoned on her like a great big neon sign. But how was she supposed to sit across a narrow space from such a big man and not touch him? She tensed as the waitress arrived with their food, giving her a brief respite. Did he know? Had he guessed? She couldn't tell. 'You pick a topic. You start,' she said, as soon as the waitress had left them.

'I would have thought my topic was obvious.'

'Really?' She frowned. 'Not to me.'

'My topic's you, Emma.' Luc focused his whole attention on her. 'I want you, Emma.' Her throat instantly felt as if it was in a noose. 'I want you in my bed,' Luc continued smoothly.

Be sensible. *This is not a romantic moment*, she warned herself. Luc had spoken with about as much emotion as he had used to give their order for toast.

'I want you in my bed because I enjoyed you,' he said, confirming this as he angled his chin to direct a stare into her eyes. 'I can't stay in Scotland for much longer, so I want you to come back with me to Brazil.'

'To Brazil,' she breathed.

'That is where I live most of the year.'

'Yes, I know,' she said faintly, 'but I won't be your mistress.'

Luc smiled wryly. 'I wasn't thinking of anything quite so permanent—and you've made it clear you wouldn't want that. I always had you pegged as a career girl, which is why you've thrown me by working here.' He glanced out of the window. 'I can give you a job in Brazil and look after you for as long as—'

'You want me?' she supplied.

The humour left his eyes. 'You make it sound so cold-blooded.'

'Isn't it? You're paying me to sleep with you.'

'Don't put it so crudely.'

'How would you put it?'

'I would say we were both seizing the moment and making the most of it for as long as it lasts. You would never have to worry about anything again. You'd never have to work another day in your life, if you didn't want to. And you'd get to sleep with me every night.' He laughed.

Emma didn't laugh. 'Until you tire of me and throw me out.'

Luc sat back, appearing wholly at ease with his suggestion. He didn't even have the good grace to seem impatient at her comment. 'It's a great offer, Emma.'

'It's prostitution dressed up in a uniform of your choice.'

'That's harsh.'

'But it's the truth, and you can't deny it.'

Luc didn't even attempt to deny it. 'Looking at it your way, you must admit that what I'm suggesting is cost-effective.'

'What?' she exploded. 'You are totally shameless.'

'I'm just being open about the fact that I don't want you for just one night, or even a couple of nights. I want you in Brazil so I can have sex with you whenever I want.'

'That's outrageous.'

'It's honest.' He put a restraining hand on her arm when she started to get up. 'Sit,' he recommended.

People had turned to stare, and the last thing she wanted was to cause a scene. 'If that was your idea of a joke—'

'It was no joke,' Lucas assured her.

She was lost for words. She couldn't believe that even Luc could be so brazen when it came to spelling out his sexual shopping list. There was no love involved. It was a cold-blooded proposition made by a man who could buy anything he wanted. Luc was just making a bid for another item on his list.

'I enjoyed you in London,' he said, confirming this. 'I want to enjoy you again. What's so strange about that?' He shrugged. 'You're not exactly going to miss much here—no career prospects. No lifestyle. No nothing. Why not take a chance, Emma, and come with me? You enjoyed me pleasuring you. Why pretend that's not what you want?'

Her body tensed at his words, betraying her with pleasure that pulsed low and insistently when she wanted to snarl at him that his suggestion was the most insulting thing she'd ever heard in her life.

'Yes?' Luc prompted as she shifted position. 'Does your discomfort signify yes?'

'It means no,' she stated firmly, gathering what little remained of her senses. 'It means you've made me feel more uncomfortable in public than I ever have, and that's nothing to be proud of.'

'I've made you feel something,' he agreed, seeming not in the least bit perturbed. 'And that's a good thing, as far as I can tell. You've locked yourself away, Emma—and in more ways than one.'

'You could at least have pretended.'

'What? Been less blunt for the sake of good manners? I think we're past that, aren't we, Emma? Or would you prefer me to invite you to Brazil for a cultural tour?'

Luc had no intention of pretending that he wanted her for anything other than sex. And if he was after points for honesty, he could go take a hike.

'Come on, Emma,' he coaxed her in a softer tone, leaning over the table. 'I have a big appetite and so do you—and waiting to be fed doesn't suit me.'

For the second time during breakfast she was lost for words. She had no strategies to deal with

Luc. She doubted there were any. So acquire some fast, Emma, told herself fiercely.

Standing up, she flashed a smile at the lady behind the counter as she put down enough money to cover their meal, including a generous tip. 'See you soon,' she called out brightly as she headed for the door. Luc's proposition might have brought memories flooding back, but no way was she selling out to the highest bidder.

Not even the father of her baby could derail her from her career goal. She would make a future for herself and for her child—and she'd do that without sleeping with Luc. She waited for the lights to turn green and then started to stalk across the road—

She'd barely taken a step when she hit a patch of ice and her legs flew from under her. It was only thanks to two strong arms catching hold of her just in time that she was saved from possible serious harm. She flashed a glance up, but she already knew who had saved her. She would know that grip, those hands, that strength, that control anywhere. 'Thank you,' she managed, as she caught her breath.

Steadying her on her feet, Luc brushed the hair from her eyes and straightened her scarf, and then he stood back. Briefly, she saw a look in his eyes that said, *Know that I will not allow you to get away from me a second time*, but just as quickly it was gone. And then he laughed. Of course he laughed. This was all just a game to Luc.

'You are impossible,' she flashed angrily. 'I hope you realise that.'

'Oh, I do,' he agreed. His powerful shoulders eased in an unconcerned shrug. 'You don't have to give me your answer right away.'

'Oh, please,' she insisted. 'Let me give it to you now.' She drew a breath and then fired at him, 'No.'

Easing onto one hip, he assured her, 'You'll change your mind. I'll give you twenty-four hours to think about it.'

'I don't need time to think about it. What do I have to say to convince you?' She raked her hair with frustration. 'You might not think I've got much here, but I've got my pride, and I've got a life here. I won't be scrubbing floors for ever. I have plans.'

'And so do I,' Luc interrupted. 'I have plans for you.'

'I think I know what they are.'

'And I think you're wrong. Why don't you give me a chance to explain?'

'Because your plans belong in the Dark Ages when men thought women were glad to hear they would never have to work another day in their life, while I happen to live in the real world, where women are quite capable of getting along without men.'

'Without men?' He smiled. 'Not you, Emma. But, as it happens, making your own way in the world is exactly what I'm talking about—but if you don't want to hear my suggestion...' Shoving his hands in his pockets, Luc strolled alongside her as she hurried back to the hotel. 'I'm not going to talk about it now, because I want you with a clear head when I do. So you're going to take a rest now, and then we'll have lunch and talk this through again without emotion.'

She stopped dead. 'Have you listened to a word I've said?'

'I've listened to everything you've said,' Luc assured her, 'and I'm entitled to my opinion. You have to take better care of yourself, Emma. You look wrecked. You're too pale. You're overworked, and you're getting nowhere fast.'

'I've heard enough,' she said as she brushed past him.

'You're wasting time, Emma. I will wear you down.'

'Oh…' She laughed. 'You and the housekeeper here are both determined to wear me out, or down, it seems to me.' She stopped outside the hotel gates. 'Get this through your head, Luc. Whatever it is you've got planned, it isn't going to happen so don't waste your time. It might be customary in the world you inhabit to buy any woman who takes your fancy, but in my world women don't sell themselves to a man.'

'Don't worry, I'll make sure you earn your keep.'

He said this softly, but there was a dangerous glint in his eyes. Shaking her head with incredulity, as if that could blank out the sight of the attractive crease that appeared in Luc's ridiculously handsome face, she gave a thought to the bigger picture. She had to tell him. She couldn't risk alienating him completely. Maybe lunch would work. If they had an unemotional meeting over food, it could be the right moment to tell him. 'We do have to talk,' she admitted, 'just to set you straight once and for all, but only if you promise not to bring up the subject of my becoming your mistress again.'

His smile flashed heat from the top of her head to the tips of her toes. 'As I've already explained, I don't plan anything so permanent.'

'But you want me under your power in Brazil.'

'You'd certainly be under me.'

Exasperated, she shook her head. 'Breakfast didn't work. Why should lunch be any better?

We can't even hold a civil conversation over a boiled egg.'

'Try it,' Luc suggested. 'I know you want to.'

Yes, but not for the reasons he thought. 'If you have a serious job offer for me to consider, I might be interested in visiting Brazil. Otherwise? Not a chance. And any job you offer me would have to come without strings attached. I would need a proper contract,' she stressed, struggling to blank the memories of endless pleasure at his hands as Luc studied her.

'So—lunch?' he said, jolting her back to reality. 'I still owe you for breakfast, remember?'

'I paid because I don't want to feel I owe you anything. You don't have to pay me back,' she said when Luc began to speak. 'I don't need your money, Luc. And I don't need you.'

'But you want me,' he said, confident as ever.

She hated him for being right, but knew that everything could change in the blink of an eye. Luc was being so reasonable now—so good-humoured and easygoing. But tell him about the baby and everything would change.

Face the problem now. Don't leave it to fester and grow bigger.

'Late lunch?' she suggested briskly, working out how long it would take her to rest and recover.

Luc's lips pressed down with satisfaction at her apparent climb-down. 'Are you sure you can spare the time?'

'I usually take a break for a couple of hours in the afternoon before I start work again.'

'Then it's a date,' he confirmed, all humour gone from his face, as if that were another deal signed, sealed and delivered, and there was no longer any need to work the charm.

So much for his foolproof plan, Luc concluded as he strode back to the café to pick up his car. He should have known Emma would need a different approach from other women. She wasn't on the lookout for a wealthy sponsor. She never had been. He had always taken it for granted that with his busy schedule it was more straightforward to be the provider of good things with no strings attached, but trying that approach with Emma had just nosedived spectacularly. Her refreshingly blunt responses made him laugh out loud as he mentally replayed them as he walked back along the ice-bound streets. His libido would have to wait until he came up with a better offer, like a serious job she really would be a fool to refuse. Patience, he told himself sensibly. He had business to finish in town, and not too long to wait until he saw Emma again and could hit her with a revised proposition.

When his work was done, he drove back at a leisurely pace to the hotel. The first thing he did when he reached his room was to call the front desk to ask to speak to Emma.

So much for her afternoon rest!

Cursing viciously, he replaced the receiver. What now? Was she trying to kill herself? They'd informed him that, yes, Ms Fane was in the hotel, but as she was working she couldn't come to the phone. Why, when she had said she was going to take a rest, was Emma back at work? What was she trying to prove? Surely she couldn't need money so badly?

Pacing the room, he examined the facts. When her parents' criminal activities had come to light, the courts had confiscated everything they'd owned, so Emma had inherited nothing, but she was a capable woman who didn't strike him as being dependent on anyone, let alone the parents who, by all accounts, had never shown much interest in her.

He stared out of the window at the grey scene below. Traffic was barely moving, and what few people were brave enough to venture out on foot were bundled up in what appeared to be every heavy winter garment they possessed. His thoughts turned to Emma with the sultry sun of Brazil on her face.

She would love Brazil.

CHAPTER FIVE

'HE DID WHAT?' Emma demanded, her voice tight with shock. She was facing the housekeeper over the gleaming stainless-steel counters in the kitchen, which Emma had just cleaned.

'Mr Marcelos has asked for you to be released from your duties this afternoon, and I've said yes,' the housekeeper informed Emma. 'He asked for you most particularly—he said no one else would do.'

The housekeeper was avid for gossip, Emma concluded as the older woman's gaze sharpened on her face. 'It was good of you to offer to stand in at the last minute, Emma. I know we can always depend on you, but if this man wants to offer you a better job, I can't stop you leaving. In fact, I don't want to stop you,' the housekeeper admitted in a surprising moment of empathy.

'Maybe you'll have the chance to go places that I never had. You should at least find out what he's got in mind. You shouldn't let yourself be trapped in a small place like this. A young woman like you should spread your wings.'

Emma had never heard the housekeeper say so much to her in one outburst before. It made her feel ungrateful that she could turn down an opportunity without even considering it.

'You used to work for him, didn't you?' the housekeeper pressed.

'Yes. It's on my CV. I worked for the Marcelos hotel chain in London.'

'And now fate has brought the owner of that hotel chain back into your life. You can't ignore a sign like that.'

'The chance of a job working for Senhor Marcelos's hotel chain has cropped up,' Emma emphasised. 'There's nothing more to it than that.'

'I don't know what you're waiting for.' The housekeeper sniffed as if she would have seized the opportunity with both hands, given half a chance.

'Yes. What are you waiting for, Emma?'

Emma swung round to see Luc standing in the doorway.

'You should at least allow Mr Marcelos to tell you what he's got in mind,' the housekeeper pressed, simpering as she ogled Lucas.

Who did look amazing in a soft black cashmere sweater and jeans, but that wasn't a good enough reason to massage his ego, Emma thought. She had a pretty good idea what Lucas had in mind. Judging by his expression his latest suggestion would be similar to the first, and it would be far better to deal with him away from prying eyes. Putting her cloths and cleaning products away, she washed her hands and then allowed the housekeeper to chivvy her out of the kitchen.

'You can't keep a man like Mr Marcelos waiting,' the housekeeper insisted, with more smiles and simpering directed at Luc.

Oh, can't I? Emma's gaze clearly stated, when Luc raised an amused brow.

'Where are you taking me?' she demanded, as he shooed her up the back stairs to the lobby.

'To my suite, where you'll rest and then we'll talk.'

'Your suite?' She held back. 'I don't think so,' she protested as he called the lift. 'I'm not getting off on your floor,' she warned as the lift doors slid to, enclosing them inside the restricted space.

It was her lucky day. The elevator was crowded. At least she didn't have to face an argument with Luc when she was exhausted and at her lowest ebb, though she did feel awkward dressed in her maid's uniform, red-faced and work-worn, amongst such expensively clad guests. She smelled of carbolic, while everyone else smelled of money. French cologne for the men and expensive blends for the women; even the children emitted a strong smell of soap, but none of them stank like she did. No wonder everyone was carefully avoiding looking at her.

Except for Luc, she noticed, who was leaning back against the wall, studying her with a steady gaze. She turned her head away. She didn't want to look at him. He was one more polished reminder of the yawning gap between herself and everyone else in the elevator.

When the lift stopped and everyone got out, she told herself that she only had a couple more floors to go. Luc didn't move as they soared upwards again, but when the doors slid open he did more than stop her, he pinned her to the wall with his arm resting above her head and his body pressed up hard against hers. She wasn't going anywhere, his smiling eyes told her, and though she should hate him, be angry with him, at least, for trying to control her, his dark, amused stare was hypnotising.

'Don't fight me, Emma,' he growled in a way that reverberated through her. 'I've only got your best interests at heart. You need to rest, and if I let you out of here unescorted, how can I be sure you won't go straight back to work? To summarise, if I have to lasso you and tie you to a chair in my room, that's what I'm going to do, because you are going to take a rest before you collapse.'

He allowed the doors to slide to at that point,

and when they reached the next floor, his floor, Luc ushered her out onto the corridor. 'First you take a bath and then you sleep. You missed lunch, so I'm going to order supper to be served in the room when you wake up.'

'I'd rather just talk and then go up to my own room, if you don't mind,' she said stiffly. Yet again she was exhausted, and didn't want this to be the time when she told him. Her body was screaming for sleep. Her mind wasn't sharp. Her emotions were in tatters. This was the worst time possible to drop a bombshell like a baby into Luc's lap.

'I do mind,' he said. 'You promised me you'd rest last time, yet I found you back at work. I can't trust you to stay in your room, Emma, and I won't be responsible for you collapsing with exhaustion. I can't pretend I know why you're punishing yourself, but as a previous employer I can't stand by and allow it to carry on.'

And when she'd slept and was refreshed, she could speak to him, Emma reasoned as Luc opened the door to his room. Closing it behind them, he stood with his back to it. 'Where would you go if not here with me?'

She rolled her tired eyes. 'To my room.'

'To a cold cell in the attic,' Luc said with an impatient gesture. 'Why would you want to do that, when you've got everything here that you could possibly need? And you'll have the place to yourself.'

'To myself?' Her head shot up with surprise.

'I have some business to attend to in town.'

So when would she speak to him?

'Stop frowning, Emma. You won't be disturbed. I thought that would please you.' A genuine smile tugged at the corner of his mouth. 'And I'm willing to bet my bed is a lot more comfortable than yours.'

She couldn't deny that. The thought of trying to find a comfortable spot on her old, lumpy mattress held no appeal.

'There's a spa bath through there,' Luc went on, indicating the bathroom as if she hadn't cleaned it umpteen times.

'This I know,' she wryly.

'It's a fantastically clean bathroom,' he stressed, mocking her with his eyes. 'I'll have you know I have the best chambermaid in the area.'

He made it hard not to smile. When Luc turned it on, his charm was irresistible.

'And if you miss supper, you'll go hungry,' he pointed out. 'And, knowing you, you'll go straight back onto your next shift whether you've eaten or not. So what do you have to lose by taking time out here?'

Everything, Emma thought as she glanced at the bed.

She was still sleeping when he got back. He guessed she still had a lot of catching up to do. He'd never seen anyone look quite so exhausted. Thanking the waiter who'd brought the supper trolley, he took control and wheeled it into the room. He returned to put a 'Do Not Disturb' notice on the door and then settled down at the table to work on some papers. He'd ordered lobster salad and champagne with a view to eating whenever Emma woke up.

After about an hour he heard the sheets rustle and turned to look at her. Emma was waking slowly, like a child unsure of her surroundings. She looked so vulnerable she touched him somewhere deep. He blanked the feeling. He hadn't registered a single emotion for years beyond lust or boredom with a woman, and it was far better for both of them if he kept it that way.

Rubbing her eyes, she stared around, first in confusion and then with embarrassment and shock.

'Relax. I've been sitting here, working,' he reassured her. 'No one came near you while you were asleep.'

'Luc!' She shot up and then, realising she had fallen into bed naked after her bath, she grabbed the covers and pulled them up to her chin.

'You're in my room,' he confirmed as she stared at him warily. 'You needed to sleep. Can I get you something? Water? Juice?'

'I shouldn't be here.'

'Why?' He shrugged, speaking in the same low tone he used with his wild ponies. No sudden movements. No raised voices. It worked every time. Emma's darting gaze settled and her shoulders relaxed.

'I'm sorry.' She frowned. 'I must have been sleeping for ages. What time is it?'

He glanced at his watch. 'Nine o'clock.'

'Nine o'clock!' Grabbing the top sheet to wrap around her like a toga, she catapulted off the bed. 'My next shift started half an hour ago!'

'There isn't going to be a next shift.'

She paled, staring at him wide-eyed. 'What do you mean, there isn't a next shift?'

'You don't work here any more.'

She looked shocked and then she was angry. 'What have you done?'

'You quit,' he explained. 'I handed in your notice.'

'You did what?' Furious now, she raked her hair. 'Do you have any idea what you've done? I need this job.' There was an edge of desperation in her voice.

'And you'll have another job,' he promised evenly. 'I'll give you a job where you don't have to work all the hours under the sun. A proper job with good prospects.'

'No, Luc! No!' she fired at him, moving behind a chair as if it were a shield when he came towards her. 'You said you wanted to talk to me. You said I could use your room to rest, and that it was more comfortable than mine. What you didn't tell me was that while I was safely out of the way you would make critical decisions on my behalf that weren't yours to make.'

'Now you're properly awake we can talk,' he said steadily.

'Talk?' she demanded. 'Not before you explain to my employers that I'm not leaving here, and that this is all some terrible mistake.'

'I won't stand by and watch you destroy yourself,' he said quietly, holding her furious stare.

'What I do is none of your business,' she fired back at him. Stalking to the bathroom, she returned clad in his robe. 'You can't just walk back into my life and take it over.'

'I'm not trying to do that.' He maintained the same calm tone. 'You're an intelligent woman,

Emma. I pulled your report from the hotel in London. Everyone speaks so highly of you, so why are you still hiding away in Scotland? If the chatter about your parents bothers you, I can tell you now that it will never go away unless you stand and face it.'

'I'm not in hiding. I've come home.'

'The world's a big place, Emma. Why don't you take a look at some more of it before you make up your mind that you want to stay here?'

'The world might be a big place for you, but I don't have your resources.'

'Your world can be as big as you want it to be. Don't put false limits on your imagination.'

She laughed without humour. 'And how am I supposed to do that? And what if I'm happy here? Has it even occurred to you that not everyone wants what you want, and that some of us are happy in our own back yard? Or is this all about you, Luc? Are you trying to get me to come back to London so I'll be there at your beck and call?'

To any other woman he might have said, 'Don't flatter yourself,' but this was Emma.

'And you can stop looking at me like that right now,' she flashed furiously. 'I don't want your pity. And I can't think why else you would waste your precious time pretending you care about me, unless it's to pursue that ridiculous idea that I would be prepared to share your bed until you tire of me, and that I wouldn't even be your full-time mistress—short term, didn't you call it?'

'Do you want to be my full-time mistress?'

'Stop teasing me,' she yelled. 'That is not what I want. Anything but that.'

'I'm not teasing you. Nothing's changed. I want you to come with me when I leave Scotland. I want you in my bed.'

'And what about my future?' she demanded with a scandalised laugh. 'What type of future will I have if I'm forever trailing around after you? I won't have a future! And if you think for one minute I'd agree to that, you really are off your head. Is that clear enough for you?'

'You won't turn me down,' he said quietly, and with absolute confidence.

'Won't I?'

Emma huffed incredulously, but as she went to storm past him he caught hold of her and dragged her close. Every inch of him was pressed up hard against her. Every inch of her was soft and warm and yielding, as her stiffness and anger gave way to something else.

'Do you seriously think you only have to snap your fingers and I'll come running?' she demanded in a shaking voice.

'Yes,' he said as he smiled into her darkening eyes. 'I think exactly that.'

'No, Luc.' She slowly shook her head. 'You don't know me. I won't be controlled, and you are always trying to control me.'

'But you want me. You've tried life without me and you know how empty that is.'

'I know you're an arrogant—'

He drove his mouth down on hers, kissing her into silence. She was everything he wanted and more. She was hot. She was aroused. She was angry. They matched each other for passions. She was already moving against him in the hunt for more contact, and he knew exactly how to deal with that.

Infuriated beyond reason by frustration when he pulled away, she launched an attack, her tiny fists flailing as he brought her back and held her tight against the wall of his chest. 'Don't,' he murmured against her silky hair. 'You'll only hurt yourself.'

'I'll hurt you first,' she assured him heatedly.

She already had, he realised. Emma Fane had blasted his cold stone heart to hell. 'I would never hurt you.'

'So you say.' She whipped her face away as he brushed her mouth with his.

'I mean it,' he insisted quietly, realising he was absolutely sincere.

'Until the next woman comes along?' she demanded sceptically, staring at him with furious eyes. 'I know your track record, Luc. Everyone knows your track record. It's hardly a secret when you feature in every celebrity magazine under the sun.'

'If you think I live my life in a public forum, you don't know me at all.'

She was panting for breath—anger, not arousal, he suspected as she softened against him. 'Come with me,' he coaxed then. Cupping her chin, he brought her back to face him, and when he brushed her lips this time he felt her tremble. 'You'll achieve nothing here, except working yourself to death, when I can offer you a world of opportunity.'

'Yes,' she interrupted, her eyes wounded as she stared into his. 'But it would be your world, not mine.'

'Working double shifts as you do shouldn't be anyone's world,' he said, filled with exasperation and anger when he thought of how this hotel abused its staff. 'Killing yourself with exhaustion won't help you to forget anything.'

'Don't,' she snapped. 'Don't you dare pull that card!'

Emma had never given herself the chance to recover from the shock of her parents' death, and he knew grief couldn't be pushed aside and forgotten, and that it had to be brought out into the open, to be faced up to and dealt with. And even then, coping strategies were necessary for a long time, maybe for ever. Emma hadn't scraped the surface of her grief, but had thrown herself into his arms, and then into her work instead.

'I'm done with arguing with you,' he warned.

'And I'm finished with you,' she assured him angrily, struggling in his arms. 'Will you please let me go?'

'No,' he said flatly. 'This discussion is over.' And to prove it, he kissed her into silence.

'No. Luc!' she said when he finally released her. 'You can't get round me this time!'

'No?' he queried, kissing her neck.

She shivered and tried to pull away as he rasped his stubble gently against her tender skin. Finally, she rested her hands flat again his chest. 'You don't play fair.'

'No. I don't,' he agreed. Running his hands lightly down her back, he whispered, 'Now we eat.' He smiled to feel her tremble. Was the disappointment on her face because he'd chosen food over progressing this?

She made an angry sound. 'Do you really think I'm going to sit down and eat with you?' Her gaze flashed to the food.

'You need to eat. I'll feed you, if I have to,' he warned.

'I'm not hungry.' But her rumbling stomach gave her away.

Her hand felt so small in his as he led her to the sofa, where he told her to sit. This was quite unlike any other encounter he'd ever had with a woman and required a whole new rulebook. Emma was like a wounded animal who had come back home to Scotland, thinking she could avoid the media furore in London surrounding her parents' death, only to find the uproar was also well rooted here. She had no one to turn to. Her friends were married, or moving away, leaving her to cope with the fact that she was well and truly on her own.

She ate slowly at first, and then ravenously

without inhibition. He thought back to another night and a different appetite.

'What?' She looked at him, sensing his distraction. 'Aren't you going to eat anything? Shall I choose something for you?'

He huffed a small laugh. 'In the interests of equality, go right ahead.'

Her small gesture touched him. When she passed him the plate of food, he reached out and ran his forefinger lightly down her cheek.

CHAPTER SIX

SHE WANTED TO be angry with Luc, but he made it so difficult. He made it impossible, by being unreasonable one minute and yet so kind the next. She had so many more important things to discuss with him than whether or not they should eat. Until she reminded herself that this quiet interlude was exactly the right time to explain calmly that she was expecting his child.

'Relax,' Luc insisted, sensing her sudden tension.

It was so easy to slip back into a fantasy where they were expectant parents, sharing precious time together as they waited for the birth of their longed-for child.

'Fruit,' he said, snapping her out of the fantasy. 'You need to eat fruit for the vitamins, you're so pale. And you need the chocolate because you like it.' He slipped a chocolate-coated strawberry between her lips.

How could she not indulge in that fantasy when the man she loved was smiling into her eyes? Yes. She loved him. Crazy. Inconvenient. Fact.

It was crazy because love between them was unlikely in the extreme, and inconvenient because her feelings for Lucas always clouded her mind. 'Luc, I—'

'Not now, Emma. We're going to leave heavy discussions for another time. It's getting late and you're still tired. We will find a time to talk, but not tonight. Good?' he murmured, slipping another berry between her lips.

Everything was good, except for the opportunity to tell him being snatched away, and though Luc's eyes were warm and amused as he tempted her with the ripe fruit, she got the feeling that he was asking her another question entirely. Luc accepted no boundaries, no restrictions, and he took his freedom, along with the freedom to indulge his smallest whim, for granted. He had an enormous appetite for life that saw him zooming back and forth across the globe. He lived a privileged life she could only imagine. And while their baby meant more than life itself to her, Luc had given her no reason to be confident that he would feel the same. How was he going to take the news that he was about to become a father? 'I should get dressed.'

Luc's eyes darkened. 'Why?'

'Do I need a reason?'

Angling his chin, his mocking eyes gave her the only answer he was going to give her.

'I'm going to get dressed.' She stood, conscious that she was naked beneath the robe. And not just naked but violently aroused. Playful little pulses were throbbing between her legs, while just the abrasion of the material against her super-sensitive nipples was enough to make them pucker and strain towards him. Luc was so physical it was impossible not to respond.

She stopped on the way to the bathroom, shivers streaking down her spine knowing Luc was behind her. His heat strengthened the pulses tempting her, making them impossible to ignore.

Could she resist him? However many times her mind screamed caution, she couldn't stop her body craving his touch. It didn't help that every little detail of their wild night in London had led to the creation of a child, and that, far from acting as a warning that might prevent her from responding to him, that fact appealed to some primal instinct that demanded she must continually reinforce the relationship with her mate.

Breath caught in her throat as Luc towered over her. He made her feel small and protected, and made her body glow with every expectation of being pleasured again.

'You're beautiful,' he murmured in a husky drawl.

She inhaled sharply as he pushed the robe from her shoulders and let it drop. Cupping her breasts, he made breathing difficult as he worked some magic with his hands. Her nipples responded instantly to his touch, and the sensation was spectacular. In her mind she was back in London, with Luc leaning over her, exhaling shakily as he moved steadily, rhythmically, deep inside her. She had missed this, missed him. Luc knew just how to touch her. He was sensitive to her every need, and her body shook with longing for him. When he scored the tips of her nipples very lightly with his thumbnails she was lost.

'It's been too long, Emma.'

'Yes,' she agreed. Her lips were dry. She licked them and could remember how swollen they had been from his kisses. She wanted more kisses, more touches, more of everything; her body ached for him. She wanted him deep inside her. She wanted him to possess her, to hold her down and pleasure her as he had done then. She could remember exactly how it had felt to have him fill her, and how he had withdrawn slowly and completely, only to plunge back hard. She wanted that extreme of pleasure again, and she wanted it now.

'Yes?' Luc queried, his black eyes smiling into hers.

'Yes,' she said, remembering how he'd taken her so firmly against a wall he'd driven her up it with every stroke. She could still remember the pleasure and her screams of excited release, and then Luc soothing her down again.

'What?' he murmured, smiling against her mouth when she sighed and closed her eyes. 'Are you remembering?'

How did he know?

His hands moved firmly over the swell of her belly and down the insides of her thighs, making her core yearn for him, though he was careful to miss every part of her that craved him. She gulped in some much-needed air, and even widened her stance a little, only to admit to herself that Luc was the master of frustration, as well as the master of seduction. He knew just how to bring her to the brink and keep her hovering there. A firmer touch in the right place was all it would take. Tension was building—becoming unsustainable. She was like an overwound spring. Covering his hands with hers, she refused to wait and, applying more pressure, she rocked her body into his.

He nudged her away.

'Why?'

Ignoring her cry of desperation, he showed her why. Dipping his head, he took her nipple into his mouth and suckled it firmly, whilst torturing the other between his thumb and forefinger. The extremes of pleasure transferred straight to her core, while Luc watched every reaction, and read every hungry little thought in her head, until finally he lifted her into his arms and carried her to the bed.

She shivered as his mouth left a trail of sensation over her neck, her ear, her eyelids, and finally her mouth, by which time she was lost to reason. Teasing her with his tongue, he demanded full access to her mouth. His arms pinioned her like steel bars on either side of her body, holding her in place while he plundered her mouth and she whimpered shamelessly with need. Then, lowering himself, he tightened his arms around her. His tongue circled hers, plunging deep and withdrawing slowly in a mind-numbing sequence of reminders of another night, another act—

'Not yet,' he instructed when her body tensed.

How could she hold back when Luc had brought

her to the edge with nothing more than a kiss and a suggestion?

'Soon,' he promised, reading her with his usual ease.

'Please,' she said, her eyes entreating him.

'How badly do you want this, Emma?'

She couldn't answer him. She was wholly focused on sensation. Luc had positioned himself between her thighs and had pushed them apart, leaving her exposed, swollen and ready for him. Lifting her legs, he rested them on the wide spread of his shoulders. 'Rest back on the pillows,' he ordered. 'Relax and let me do all the work. You're so aroused.'

His tone was appreciative as he stared down. A smile hovered around his mouth as she dragged in a ragged breath. Pressing her thighs even further apart, he dipped his head to deliver new levels of pleasure. Holding him close, she worked her body frantically against his mouth until she was there…almost there. Hovering suspended in Luc's erotic net, she was ready to fall. The world shimmered around her. She was so close to the edge, she didn't know if she could hold on, but Luc was too skilled to indulge her so quickly, and knew exactly when to pull back.

'Don't tease me,' she begged, lacing her hands through his hair.

Reaching up, he cupped her breasts, shifting his hands as he enclosed them.

She flinched—just a little, but enough to alert him to the fact that her breasts were really tender, and maybe they had filled out a little too. She froze as he stilled. She'd been so engrossed in passion and need she hadn't even considered the first and, to date, the only sign that she was pregnant.

'Emma?' Lifting his head, Luc stared at her. For a moment his expression didn't change, but then it did and time froze as they stared at each other in silence.

Grabbing a cover, she swung out of bed. Instinct demanded that she be on her feet when she faced him.

Luc broke the silence first. 'Why didn't you tell me?'

Her stomach clenched with apprehension. Luc had changed in an instant from powerfully seductive to cold and mistrustful. Her throat tightened with dread. It wasn't supposed to be like this. And this was all her fault. She should have told him long before now. It was no excuse to say the opportunity had never come. Standing motionless with his back turned to her, Luc's tension frightened her. He was so powerful her imagination was hard at work. He might decide to take their child from her. He might decide to prove she was an unfit mother by fighting her through the courts, and how could she afford to fight him?

She had to calm down. That was the first step. Then she had to find a way to calm Luc, but she didn't know this man. Even his back was hostile. Their friendship had been tenuous at best, and now it was destroyed. She covered herself with the sheet. Somehow she had to make this right, but Luc was in no mood to listen.

'Don't play the fool with me, Emma. When were you going to tell me? Ever?' he demanded, swinging round. His furious stare drilled into hers. 'Or did you want me well and truly hooked before you decided to mention it?'

'No! Of course not.'

'And I'm supposed to believe this is my child?'

'I wouldn't lie to you where my child is concerned.'

'I don't know what to think. I don't know you at all.'

He was right. They didn't know each other. Why wouldn't Luc think the worst of her? She hadn't exactly played hard to get in London. Or here, for that matter. And Luc had never pretended to want anything but sex. She could accept he was shocked. The last thing he was expecting was that their casual fling would take such a life-changing turn.

'I'm going to take a shower.' His muscles rippled with hostility as he turned his back. 'There's another bathroom over there. Use it, and get out.'

To say he was shocked by his discovery would be massively understating the case. He was tempted

to believe it was his baby. He doubted Emma
would lie to him where a child was concerned.
She had never been the type to take advantage of
a situation. It was usually the other way round,
with the situation taking advantage of Emma.

Adjusting the shower to ice-cold, he turned his
face up to the stinging spray. Close relationships
didn't work for him. He had never pretended otherwise. His plan had been to offer Emma a deal
she couldn't refuse—the best training in the hotel
industry, and enough money to start her own
business, if that was what she wanted. It would
be the pay-off for pleasure—cheap at the price
for both of them. No strings attached. No regrets.
No consequences on either side.

But now?

Now a child was involved and that changed
everything. At some deep primal level he knew
without doubt that he was the father, and that
linked him to Emma for all time. The child
linked them. His whole thinking had been forced
to change in an instant. Feelings he had brutally
pushed aside for years had come flooding back.

Two people creating a new life had touched him somewhere deep. He was going to be a father, and it was inconceivable to him that any child of his should grow up not knowing him. He would not be denied the pleasure of sharing everything he had to give as he watched that child grow and flourish.

The child would have to live with him. That much was clear.

Then he remembered his own childhood and his own beloved mother, who had cared for him in spite of the fact that she suffered under the heel of his father. Was he going to deny his own child that same love and commitment—that caring and nurturing love that only a mother could give?

She was frozen to the spot, standing in the bathroom, breathing, just about. She had taken a shower on autopilot, barely registering whether the water was hot or cold. This was not supposed to be happening. This was her worst nightmare come true. She had wanted to be the one in control, the one to tell Luc about the baby when they were both relaxed and Luc was receptive to news that would change his life. It was too late for that now. The news had hit him like a bolt from the blue, and she didn't need Luc to tell her that he didn't want this. Why would Luc want his life to change when he had everything? He controlled everything. Or he had done until she'd come along and her pregnancy became the one thing in his life over which Luc had no control.

'Emma...'

She flinched as he hammered on the door. Her time was up. His voice was hostile. She doubted they could ever get past this.

Maybe not, but this was her body and her choice to make. This was one occasion when she was in charge, not Luc. Whatever he said or did now, she would never regret her pregnancy. They had both created a child, and she accepted her responsibility fully and gladly, and if Luc couldn't bring himself to do the same, then that was up to him. Pulling on her clothes fast, she tidied up the bathroom and then opened the door. Luc was standing by the window with his back turned to her. When he heard the door open he swung around.

'How much do you want, Emma?'

His first question hit her like a blow. Lifting her chin, she met his hostile stare steadily. 'I don't want anything from you.'

'Really?' One ebony brow lifted. 'You'll be the first person in my experience who doesn't want something from me.'

'How sad to always have to doubt other people's motives. Is that what wealth does to you, Luc?'

'You don't know what you're talking about.'

'And I can't talk to you while you're in this mood.'

'Why?' Luc said coldly. 'Are you afraid it will get you nowhere?'

'I'm not afraid of anything. We're both coming to terms with a radically changed future, but be in no doubt that I will protect my child, and my right to be with that child, with the last breath in my body.'

Luc ripped into her. 'I should have known when

I first saw you at the wedding party that night—your evasive manner, your shock at seeing me. All it would have taken was a quick calculation on my part, but I didn't want to see what was in front of my eyes—'

'I've had enough. I'm not here to be judged by a man who was happy enough to bed me, but who rejects the consequences. I can only assume that when you saw me at the wedding your brain was below your belt at the time.'

Luc reared back with surprise. The last thing he had expected had been for her to take him on. Lucas Marcelos versus Emma Fane, chambermaid? No contest, he must have thought. No contest? She'd be a mother soon. He'd better get used to that idea, and do some research while he was at it, on the lengths a mother would go to in order to protect her child.

'I'll need proof that your baby is mine,' he grated out.

'I'd expect nothing less,' she said coldly. 'I used protection. What went wrong?'

When pulling rank had failed, Luc had turned

to interrogating her, but her fighting spirit was back full force, and she was ready for him. 'Do I really need to tell you what went wrong? I may not have your extensive experience of such things, but as two adults surely we both know that protection isn't foolproof, and on this occasion it failed.'

'Clearly.' A muscle flicked in his jaw as he regarded her coldly. 'Well, we are where we are, so I will tell you what's going to happen next.'

'No, you won't,' she argued firmly. 'This is one occasion where you don't decide. This is my body and my baby—'

'Our baby, according to you,' he fired back.

'Our baby,' she conceded. 'There is no blame here, Luc. We're both equally responsible for this child, and both equally invested in its future.' She hoped that was true, and something in Luc's eyes said he did want to be part of this, though whether that was a good thing, right now she couldn't tell.

For all that he was a notorious playboy, Lucas Marcelos was famous for his loyalty—to his friends, to his polo team and to the staff who worked for him. She had no reason to suppose he wouldn't be equally invested in the welfare of his child. She had never heard anyone say a bad word about him. Her only worry was that Lucas would take his sense of responsibility to the nth degree, and that once he was satisfied he was the father of her child he would demand complete control.

CHAPTER SEVEN

HIDING HER CONCERN, she tried to reason with him. 'I'm truly sorry I couldn't tell you sooner, but the right moment never came.'

'The right moment?' Luc scoffed. 'And when would that have been?'

'I don't know,' Emma said honestly. 'But I do know I didn't want it to be like this, with both of us angry and upset. But we still have to find a way forward.'

'We?' He practically laughed in her face. '*We* will decide how to play this? How are you going to raise a child? At the hotel in your freezing box room in the attic?'

'I'm lucky to have a roof over my head. And I won't live here for ever. I'm saving each week to provide a better life—'

'Pennies,' he scorned. 'You're saving pennies

a week as you work yourself to death. How will you care for a child when you've made yourself ill?'

'The hotel is opening a crèche—'

'A hotel crèche for my child?'

'Why not, Lucas? It's good enough for your staff,' she blazed back.

For once, he couldn't disagree, but he soon returned to his original point. 'No child of mine is going to be brought up in one room.'

'Why is your child so different from millions of others?'

'I'm surprised you need to ask. If you're carrying my child, you know I can offer it so much more than you can.'

'More love than I can?' As far as material things were concerned, he was right, but how much did a child really need in the way of luxury? Surely love and warmth and food was enough for any child?

'I'm not talking about love,' he said impatiently. 'I'm talking about trying to bring a child up here at a hotel in the middle of nowhere.' He shook his head angrily as he glanced around. 'Not a chance any child of mine is going to be raised in a place like this.'

'Strange, when I believe your ranch is in the wilds of Brazil.' Iron will alone forced her voice to remain steady.

'That's different.'

'How is it different, Luc?'

'You would only have to see my ranch to know.'

It would be palatial. She could hardly imagine he lived in a broken-down shack. He would employ an army of staff, amongst whom there would be many only too pleased to care for Luc's child. Everything about him screamed money and power, and, from what she'd heard, Luc had homes in London and New York, as well as the ranch. And there was a rumour racing around the hotel that he had just bought a castle in Scotland.

'What are you thinking now?' he demanded suspiciously. 'Are you trying to tot up my worth?'

'If that's the only way you can put a value on yourself, I feel sorry for you, Luc. There's a lot more to life than money and possessions.'

'Says the chambermaid with nothing.'

'Says the chambermaid who doesn't want anything from you—who never has—and who, the more I hear you speak, cannot imagine that you have anything to offer me, or my child.'

'Except several homes.'

'So our child can be batted back and forth between them? I don't think that counts as a plus. Do you?'

'You don't even know where you belong,' he countered. 'You left here for London, and now you're back again you're still not happy.'

Emma's head snapped up. 'That's a cheap shot and you know it. The one thing I do know is that I can give my child a much better childhood than either of us had—'

'What do you know about my life?' He laughed.

'Nothing. I can only imagine that it's made you what you are today. My early life taught me self-reliance, while something about yours has made you bitter and cold, so I'm guessing there isn't that much difference between us, whatever you say. And I don't believe children care too much about the setting they're brought up in, so long as they have the essentials of life, along with security and love.'

'Can you even provide the essentials?'

'Along with love and a lifetime of commitment?' She raised her chin to stare him in the eyes. 'Yes, I can.'

'You're deluding yourself, Emma, if you think I'll let you take control of this situation.'

'My child isn't a situation. It's a human being and I love it already. Just because my parents were addicts and criminals doesn't mean I've grown up the same way. Or are you saying I'm just not the right sort? Is it my bank balance or my background that's worrying you, Luc? Am I just not the type you're used to meeting in the exalted circles in which you mix?'

For a moment he seemed genuinely perplexed. 'I have never thought like that.'

'Then don't act like a jerk. Just because I don't breathe the same rarefied air as you, it doesn't mean I don't have the same aspirations for my child.'

The silence was so sudden it rang in her ears until Luc said quietly, 'Have you finished?'

'I haven't even got warmed up yet,' she assured him, firming her jaw.

'So you're going to hide in Scotland, instead of continuing your training? And that, as we both know, can only benefit your child,' he scoffed. 'Know this, Emma. That isn't going to happen.'

Lifting her chin, she glared into his eyes. 'This is something we have to decide together.'

With an impatient shake of his head Luc growled, 'Well, I won't do that here.'

She relaxed a little. At last they agreed on something. Neutral territory would be better. They couldn't stay here with the room ringing with their anger. 'Where?' she said, calming down. 'I'll meet you anywhere.'

'Brazil,' Luc stated coldly. 'We'll discuss this in Brazil.'

'You can't be serious.'

'Why not? Brazil's my home. That's where I have decided to discuss this. You owe me that much, Emma. If nothing else, you should see the other side of your child's heritage. If not for you, then for your baby.'

However much she fought against it, what Luc said made sense. She couldn't deny there was another side to her baby's heritage, but panic was already curling inside her at the thought of trekking halfway across the world with a man as hostile towards her as Luc. It had been hard enough going to London. She wasn't an adventurer like Lizzie and Danny. She hadn't been further away from home than Luc's hotel, and even that time seemed a lifetime away. Once she was in Brazil she would be under Luc's control. She'd have no friends, no one to call on.

'We can talk here just as well,' she insisted.

'Let me put it another way,' Luc suggested. 'You come back to Brazil with me, or, if this child proves to be mine, I will have it taken from you when it's born.'

'You can't do that.'

'Are you willing to take that chance?'

She wasn't willing to take any chances where her baby was concerned, and there was steely

determination in Luc's eyes. He had all the resources in the world to make good on his threat
and she had none to fight him. And if by some
miracle she could take him on, did she really
want to put her child in the centre of its parents'
battleground?

'If you can suggest an alternative plan, go right
ahead,' Luc said as he waited for her to speak.

'My plan wouldn't involve a trip to Brazil.'

'Then your plan isn't an option,' he said flatly.
'You're very quick to tell me what you won't do.
Why don't you try telling me what you will do?'

'What every other single mother would do.'

'But you're not like them, Emma, because you
put me in the frame.'

'Are you saying I shouldn't have told you?'

'You didn't say anything until I challenged
you,' Luc reminded her.

This was all going so badly wrong. She had
thought she could stay in Scotland and work after
the birth, safe in the knowledge that her child was
close by in the hotel crèche. Beyond telling Luc
he was the father of her baby, she hadn't thought

much further than that. She had never imagined he would want to be involved to this extent.

'I'll start making plans,' he said, moving towards the door.

'What sort of plans? I haven't given you a decision yet.'

'My plans to fly home to Brazil,' he said, frowning. 'You'll come with me, of course. You'll be informed when we're leaving.'

'No, Luc—' She stopped. The expression on his hard, autocratic face chilled her to the bone. What was she going to do? Say no to him? Did she really want a life for her child where its mother was always looking over her shoulder to see if Luc was coming to claim her baby, or was she going to sort this out now?

'Anything more you have to say to me can be said in Brazil,' Luc informed her.

'I'm not going anywhere until we talk. This isn't some business deal where you can reasonably request a change of venue. We'll talk here, and then I'll decide if I'm going to travel halfway across the world with you.'

'I can't force you into anything,' he confirmed, 'so if you're happy to ignore all the things your child is going to benefit from in Brazil, I can't do much about it.' He shrugged. 'But I would have thought that as a mother you would at least want to familiarise yourself with the country where your child is going to live.'

'My child will live with me,' she exclaimed, panic-stricken.

'Which is why I intend to repeat my offer of a job,' Luc informed her coolly. 'And this time I suggest you listen carefully to my proposal before you turn it down.'

Her head was reeling. She couldn't take it in. Just when she thought she had everything sorted out in her head, Luc threw a curveball. 'You're offering me a job in Brazil?'

'I don't know what else you think I could mean. You proved satisfactory in London, so why wouldn't you prove satisfactory in Brazil?'

Satisfactory? Was he talking about her satisfaction rating as a chambermaid or in his bed? Luc's stare didn't waver. He had no intention of dressing it up. Whatever he was talking about, she was satisfactory, no more, no less.

'Don't you think you'd better go and start packing?' he prompted impatiently.

'I've got no intention—' She stopped as he turned away to pick up the phone. Luc wasn't even listening to her. He was arranging a flight to Brazil.

Bundled up warmly in coat, scarf and woolly hat, Emma waited outside the hotel for Luc with her single battered suitcase. He arrived, frowning like an avenging angel, looking, as always, as if he'd just stepped out of the pages of a magazine. Dark jacket. Blue jeans. Heavy boots.

'Where wcre you? I looked for you inside.' Turning away impatiently before she had a chance to answer, he tipped the man who had brought up his car. 'Why did you carry your own suitcase?' he demanded. 'Why are you standing in the cold? There's no need to make yourself a martyr, Emma.'

'I'm not a martyr. I'm self-sufficient,' she said,

biting her tongue on everything else she would like to say. But Luc was right about the cold. It was freezing. The snow was drifting down and there were inches of ice beneath her feet, but she'd had to get out of the suffocating atmosphere of the hotel and breathe some clean, fresh air. She had left with a surprisingly good reference, and had been told she could come back at any time. Once again Luc had smoothed the path for her, whether she'd wanted him to or not. And now he took charge of her suitcase and helped her into the car.

He drove with confidence over the icy roads to the airport where his private jet was waiting. 'Are you warm enough?' he asked, as she hugged herself for comfort at the thought of the long trip ahead of her and its unknowable outcome.

'Yes, thank you.'

Everything was happening so fast she felt as if the little control she still had was slipping away like sand through her fingers.

'I'm surprised you're not more enthusiastic,' he commented as a fresh blanket of snow came

tumbling down. 'Rio,' he murmured, as if landing in his own country couldn't come fast enough
for him. 'Sunshine, samba and the best beaches
in the world.'

Luc was a true son of heat and passion, Emma
reflected, her stomach tightening on the thought,
while she was better here in ice and snow, never
allowing her passions to be roused. A thought
that niggled at her when Luc went on to explain
that she would be working at his flagship hotel,
which was tempting, though she'd be right under
his nose.

'It's a job with real prospects, Emma—a managerial position.'

'What?' She questioned this, feeling she wasn't
ready for such a responsible position. When she'd
left London she had only been halfway through
her training course. A job in management was
still several years away for her.

Luc chose not to answer, and she thought she
knew why. He'd moved on from telling her that
she would never have to work again in her life
to offering her a job suited to her position as the

mother of his child. The owner of such a prestigious hotel chain could hardly be associated with a girl who scrubbed floors. But this proposition didn't suit her any better than the last. 'I'd rather be myself from the off,' she said, 'which means starting at the bottom and working my way up.'

'If you're having my child you'll do as I say.'

'It doesn't work like that, Luc.' But that was her only qualification for a job in management, Emma thought, biting her tongue on the angry words she couldn't say to him now that Luc had stopped the car and got out. He had parked in front of the steps of his sleek executive jet. This was his life. Yes, and for a short time she'd be touching the fringes of it, and during that time she would make the best of every opportunity and work her socks off to win people over. She had always landed jobs fair and square in the past, and she had no intention of being paraded in public as Luc's latest girlfriend, the woman he'd promoted above her capabilities just because she pleased him in bed.

'What?' he asked, as she hovered at the foot of the steps.

She glanced up into the unreasonably handsome face that she'd seen in so many different moods. There was only coldness and resolve now, laced with impatience as Luc waited for her to mount the steps. No one went against Lucas Marcelos. No one dared.

'Hurry,' he prompted. 'I don't know why you're hesitating when you will have everything you need in Brazil.'

But would she have her freedom? Emma wondered.

CHAPTER EIGHT

NOW SHE WAS about to leave Scotland, it had occurred to her that once she set foot inside Luc's
jet she would be entering his world and leaving
her world behind.

'Let me help,' he said.

His sudden solicitude wasn't for any other reason than that he was as eager to leave Scotland as
she was to stay. He was talking to her as he might
talk to one of his brood mares on the pampas, a
creature that must be soothed before it could be
coaxed to go anywhere but a creature that would
inevitably do exactly as he said.

'What happens when I've given birth to our
child?' she asked quietly, still with her feet firmly
rooted on Scottish soil.

Luc's stare flickered. 'Nothing. Not right away.'

So like that brood mare she would be allowed

to wean her child, at which stage her baby would be taken away from her and she would be superfluous, and Luc would get rid of her. How different would that make her from her parents, who had never wanted her and who had passed her around? Was she going to let that happen to her own child? Or was she going to channel the grief she still felt at their wasted lives into a positive force for the good of her baby?

'You can make your time in Brazil pleasant or not, Emma,' Luc said, shifting position impatiently. 'It's in your hands entirely.'

Was it? As long as she made her mind up fast, she suspected, and in his favour, of course. Luc was shrewdly playing her, making it sound as if she would be in control, when they both knew it was he who held the reins. For now.

Seeing the cabin staff waiting patiently for them at the top of the steps, she asked the final question on her mind. 'Will I be expected to share your bed in Brazil?'

For the first time since he'd found out about

their baby a glimmer of humour flashed into Luc's eyes. 'Do you want to?'

She knew at once he still wanted her. God help her, she wanted him too. There was no concern in his manner as he ran up the steps to greet the waiting crew. Luc was so sure of the eventual outcome, why would he feel any concern?

'Emma. Come and meet everyone.'

She was surprised to be included in the warm greetings at the top of the steps, but was glad of it, and hurried to shake hands.

And so he had got her out of Scotland. It had been that easy, she realised ruefully as the friendly cabin staff ushered her inside the jet. She didn't need to look at Luc to see the gleam of triumph in his eyes. She knew it would be there. Where persuasion had failed him, he'd used her innate good manners against her to achieve the result he wanted. As Luc left her to complete the preflight checks, his cabin staff ushered her to her seat, which looked more like a comfortable armchair than a necessary perch on a jet. It was flanked by a magazine rack, a drinks bar, a selection of tempting nibbles, and even a tray holding high-end beauty products for her to indulge in during the flight. Luc looked in on her briefly as she was trying to settle into her glitzy surroundings.

'There are some new clothes for you in the bedroom at the back of the plane,' he said, killing her smile. Nothing had been overlooked, it seemed, and she was slightly offended that the clothes she had chosen to wear didn't pass muster, though she could accept that she hardly looked like managerial material in her beat-up coat. And it would be far too heavy to wear in Brazil, she reasoned, common-sensing herself out of the embarrassment.

'There's a bathroom too, so you can freshen up any time you want.'

'Thank you.'

Luc stood framed in the doorway to the cockpit, watching her for a moment. His face was in shadow. His arm was resting on the door. She couldn't read his expression, and had to remind herself that this wasn't about her pride but about an unborn child. *Their child.* However incredible that seemed, she smiled up at the waiting cabin crew, accepted an orange juice, and slipped off her sale-rail coat. Handing it over to them, she settled back.

Brazil. The warm air, the scents, the smells, the light, the sounds—Emma was dazzled from the instant she stepped onto the tarmac. Even at the airport, there were the smiles of the people, the music of a samba blaring from a passing truck, and the unaccustomed sunshine. She couldn't deny it was a happy start to an uncertain trip. They had landed at Santos Dumont airport in the centre of the city, with the jet seeming to scrape the top of the buildings as it came in to land. The famous landmarks—Sugar Loaf, the endless strip of ivory sand and the aquamarine sea—so familiar from postcards and travel programmes, had unfolded to her wide-eyed gaze beneath the brilliant white wings of the jet. And now she was here—

'Ready?' Luc demanded curtly as a sleek black limousine drew up.

There was no tedious protocol for him. An official had checked their passports on the aircraft so they could disembark without delay and be whisked away. It had been a long flight, during which she'd slept fitfully, waking now and then, as if she had to remind herself that she really was doing this. She had taken a shower, as Luc had suggested, before they'd landed, and had then stared in wonder at the vast array of clothes in the closet. It was the weekend, so after trying on quite a few outfits she settled for casual Capri pants and a short-sleeved top teamed with simple leather sandals. Thanking the driver who held the door for her, she climbed into the back of the limousine. It was impossible to be pessimistic. The sun was shining and her spirits soared when Luc joined her in the back. The seat was so broad there was a yawning gap between them, but at least they'd have a chance to talk. She hadn't seen him during the flight as he'd either been up on the flight deck, or sleeping in his master suite at the rear of the aircraft. She was looking forward to him pointing things out to her as they entered the centre of Rio.

That wasn't going to happen, she realised as he pulled out his phone. How could she keep on being such a fool? Nothing had changed. Luc was as distant as ever. The air was controlled. The glass panel between them and the driver was controlled. Luc's voice was controlled as he spoke rapidly in Portuguese. She shrank into a corner, feeling invisible. But she had no intention of turning back. She was here, and she was going forward whatever happened, both for her own sake and that of her child.

The Marcelos flagship hotel was a breathtaking confection of cream marble, vast tinted windows and tastefully polished bronze. She had researched the hotel online, but seeing it now beneath a flawless blue sky, surrounded by lush, colourful gardens on the fringes of a blond beach, was sensory overload. Built in the nineteen-twenties, and renovated recently to a most demanding man's specifications, every inch of the building gleamed.

'You look fine,' Luc reassured her as she smoothed suddenly damp palms down her thighs.

He was watching her. Why was she surprised? Luc was aware of everything she did, and sensitive to her every mood. For all she knew, he could read her thoughts as well.

'You're not on duty yet,' he reminded her.

Wasn't she? She was angry with herself for being so naïve. Even if her situation was about as clear as mud, she should have had more sense than to choose such a casual outfit. From the second she walked into the hotel at the owner's side she would be 'on duty' every second of every day.

Letting Luc go ahead of her, she drew in a shaking breath. Her heart thumped as she paused on the steps to gaze up at the grand façade. Towering cream walls, acres of glass, and glittering gold lettering proclaiming the Marcelos name did little to ease her anxiety. Luc's initials were everywhere. They were embroidered on the tailored coat of the uniformed doorman, and on the vast blood-red doormat under her feet, and when she entered the scented hush of the grand lobby his initials were the first thing she saw emblazoned on the front desk. Stunned by the opulence and the scale of everything around her, she stopped to stare up to the roof of an atrium that stretched to the heavens—

'Emma, there are people waiting to greet us.'

Recovering fast, she walked forward to acknowledge the line of smiles and cheery hellos. She was conscious of polite curiosity directed her way, but there was no doubt about the genuine enthusiasm for Luc. People couldn't fake that kind of warmth in their eyes. He knew everyone by name, and their passage across the football pitch–sized floor to the bank of elevators took quite some time as he spoke to each member of staff in turn.

She had done the right thing, Emma convinced herself, standing back during one of these many encounters. This was their child's heritage as much as the small village in Scotland she came from. The one thing that remained a mystery was where she fitted in. She knew nothing of Luc's personal life, and a managerial post in this hotel, however junior, was so far ahead of her in terms of training, it was a joke.

'Emma—'

She jumped, feeling annoyed with herself for needing a second prompt from Luc as the steel doors of the elevator slid open. There were no floor numbers, so this had to be the private elevator to his suite of rooms. She would soon find out. The lift was soaring up at a dizzying speed. 'Where are you taking me?'

'To your apartment.' He frowned as if he couldn't imagine where else she'd had in mind.

They stepped out onto an elegant corridor and she looked around for the type of door that might lead to the staff quarters.

'Your apartment is next to mine,' Luc explained.

How convenient.

'You will use the private elevator, as I do,' he informed her, not sparing her a glance as they walked down the corridor towards a set of elegant doors.

She had been posted in the pigeonhole marked 'job done', Emma suspected.

'You will find a security card in your apartment when I let you in,' Luc added as he opened the door. 'Don't lose it. It operates both the elevator and the door to your room. Do you have a problem with that, Emma?'

Luc had the key to her room?

Of course he had the key to her room. Luc owned the hotel. He had the key to every room. From now on she would be under his scrutiny every minute of every day.

'Don't lose that card,' he reminded her crisply. 'Freshen up. Take a rest.'

He made no attempt to follow her into her room, thank goodness. She needed a chance to take stock. 'What then?' she asked, hovering on the threshold.

'Then?' One ebony brow lifted. 'Then you will join a junior management training team tomorrow morning.'

'And that's it?' She tried to read his eyes, but

there was nothing in them to read—not for her, at least.

'Should there be more?' he queried.

Yes. She should have made better use of their time together—on the flight—on the drive here. It would have been helpful if she'd got everything ironed out about what to do and where to report in the morning before she arrived at the hotel.

'Will I see you—?' Her mouth clamped shut. Luc had already turned his back and walked away.

Okay, so she didn't need him. She wasn't helpless. She'd vowed to go it alone, and she would. Closing the door, she glanced around the cavernous suite. A bigger contrast to her small functional cell at the hotel in Scotland was hard to imagine. This was a billionaire's playroom, full of high-tech gizmos and amazing art. Floor-to-ceiling windows gave her a stunning view of the city, and there were fabulously scented flower arrangements on every surface, as well as a bottle of champagne on ice. Goodness knew what she had been expecting, but it certainly wasn't this.

She flopped down on one of the silk-covered sofas, then got up to pace. She was alone in Rio—that wasn't a problem, but she wanted to know if she should prep for her new job tomorrow. She didn't want to appear completely out of her depth when she reported for duty. Picking up her room card, she headed straight for the only other door onto the corridor.

Luc answered and seemed surprised to see her. 'May I come in?' she asked politely.

'Of course.'

He stood back. Their bodies almost touched. Heat hit the back of her neck and trickled seductively down her spine. Luc had just showered and was wearing a clean shirt. She could smell soap on him. This was the Luc she remembered from their first night in London, the distant but potentially explosive man, who was a blistering combination of searing hot passion and chilly reproof. Unfortunately for her sane and reasoning mind, this was a combination she still found irresistible.

'Is something wrong?' he queried coolly.

Everything was wrong. She was pregnant with his child. Luc's voice was totally devoid of emotion. They had never been further apart. She had come halfway around the world with him without pinning down exactly what her purpose here would be. 'I need to know, what happens next, Luc? We need to talk.'

'Now is not convenient for me.'

He had obviously made other plans, and she felt foolish for not having factored his life into her thinking. Now he'd got her here she would hardly be at the top of his agenda. But she refused to be stonewalled and sent back to her room like a naughty child. Walking deeper into the room, she turned to face him.

Luc spread his arms. 'What is it you want, Emma?'

'My timetable—my work duties?'

'You'd better sit down.'

She was rocking with jet lag, but she didn't want to sit down. Once she sank onto one of those big, cream sofas she might just fall asleep and never get up. 'No, Luc. I just want to know where to report for work tomorrow...'

Luc held up a hand to silence her as his phone rang.

She waited patiently, but when he showed no sign of ending the call she called time on asking for his assistance and walked to the door. He didn't try to stop her when she left. She wasn't even sure he noticed. Closing the door, she finally accepted that, having brought her here, Luc had lost all interest—unless she decided to sleep with him, in which case her situation might improve. He hadn't been joking when he'd said this trip would be what she made of it. It already was, and she really was alone.

CHAPTER NINE

EXHAUSTION FINALLY GOT the better of her. She took a bath, slept heavily, but she was still up at dawn. The thought of the new job, new responsibilities and not falling flat on her face was the only alarm clock she needed. It took her a moment to wake up, but once she was focused on where she was, and why, and what lay ahead of her she was a woman on a mission. She was in Rio, for goodness' sake!

Leaping out of bed, she threw back the curtains on a sunny day and the most incredible view in the world, of aquamarine sea, ivory sand and golden sunshine. Luc could be friendly and helpful, or not. She wasn't going to hang around to find out what mood he was in. She had a career to think about, and she was going to be on time for this, her first morning at her new job.

Her child needed a mother who was successful and hard-working, not a mother who was dithering about trying to decide what to do. Someone would direct her to the staff offices, and she would take it from there.

It occurred to her as she rushed about, getting ready, that other staff members were bound to jump to the wrong conclusion when they found out that she was living next to the boss. *Found out?* They probably already knew. If there was one thing that never failed to operate smoothly in a hotel, it was the gossip line. They would think—correctly, as it happened—that she was a lot more than a new trainee. She just wasn't sure what she was—or what her new colleagues would think she was.

Stop it!

She had to stop it now, or she'd lose her confidence. Switching off the shower, she grabbed a towel. She had started at a disadvantage at other jobs and made a go of it. Why should this job be any different?

Grooming was everything in the hotel business.

Taming her long red hair, she tied it back neatly and then put on her chain-store suit, the same suit she had worn for her interview in London. As Luc had pointed out on his jet, the wardrobe there had been full of clothes. The dressing room here was stuffed with every imaginable luxury outfit with matching accessories for the successful woman about town. But she wasn't a successful woman about town. Not yet. Those privileges had to be earned. And when *she* could afford it, *she* would pay for the clothes.

Luc was so wrong if he thought she could be bought with a selection of high-end suits, killer heels and accessories to die for. She might be bewitched, enthralled and tempted, but she had no intention of wearing outfits that could only put a wedge between her and her colleagues. She was going to dress to suit her position. And that position wasn't flat on her back in Luc's bed.

She took the elevator down to the ground floor. When she asked at Reception for directions to the boardroom, she was conscious of everyone trying very hard not to look at her. Thanking the desk clerk, she headed for the door he had pointed out. Quite a large group was already seated around the table when she got there. Taking in the scene at a glance, she identified one spare chair. At least there was no sign of Luc. She was relieved. She could be herself without him looming over her.

Everyone continued to stare at her as she made a beeline for the empty seat. She couldn't work out if they were expecting her. It was hard to imagine Luc overlooking a detail like that when he was so scrupulous in every other area of his life.

A thin man with thin lips waited until her bottom was almost touching the seat before telling her, 'That chair is reserved for Senhor Marcelos.'

'My apologies,' she said, shooting up again.

She had replied in English, the universal hotel language Thin Lips had used, which allowed people to confer easily with colleagues of various nationalities.

Everyone was trying even harder not to look at her and she felt bad for embarrassing them. She hadn't planned to cause such an upheaval on her first day.

'Sit here, next to me,' a girl about her own age offered, shuffling her own chair along to make space. 'Grab one of those chairs against the wall.'

One of the men jumped up, and with a smile carried the chair to the table for her. She was just thanking him when the door swung open and there stood Luc. He stared straight at her. Then he stared at the man who'd had the temerity to hold her chair. 'Problem?' he rapped.

'No problem,' she said, aiming for calm as everyone stilled around her. Her voice sounded loud in the sudden silence. It was like the moment in a drama before the gun went off, but she made a point of thanking her Good Samaritan before settling into her place. Her heart might be threatening to beat its way out of her chest at the sight of Luc looking hotter than was reasonable in a dark, impeccably tailored suit, teamed with a crisp white shirt and grey silk tie, but she had no intention of allowing this particular rampaging barbarian to know how profoundly he affected her.

She needn't have worried. Luc didn't look at her again—not for the whole of the meeting. Taking the chair she had recently vacated, he called the meeting to order and that was that.

Fine. As she had decided back in her room, she would do this with or without him. She had no intention of being browbeaten into her place.

What was her place exactly? Emma wondered as the meeting carried on without her involvement. Everyone else seemed to have a list of tasks to complete, while she had nothing.

'Excuse me,' she called out as everyone got up to leave the table. 'What are my tasks for today?'

There was an embarrassed silence, during which Thin Lips covered his mouth as if he was hiding a smile.

'Shadow me,' Luc said in a voice that rang around the room. He glanced at her impatiently, as if to suggest she shouldn't need to be told what to do when it was obvious.

To him maybe.

Hearing his tone, her colleagues had straightened their backs and adopted purposeful expres-
sions. Even Thin Lips had stopped sniggering.

'You'll soon get the hang of things,' the dark-
haired girl she had been sitting next to told Emma
discreetly.

What things? That was the question, Emma
thought as her companion introduced herself as
Karina.

'Emma,' she said with a smile.

'Everyone knows who you are,' Karina explained quietly, shooting a mischievous smile at
Emma as their colleagues filed out of the room.
'No point in pretending, is there?' Karina added
with a shrug.

'None at all,' Emma agreed, feeling she might
have found a new friend, though she would have
liked time to explain her situation as it truly was.

*Would she? Would she really? And what would
her colleagues think then?*

'What?' Luc demanded, frowning, when the
line of people waiting to have a last word with

him had finally shrunk to nil, leaving just Emma and him alone in the room.

'You said I would be shadowing you,' she reminded him.

Luc appeared to consider this, as if he had forgotten all about it, and all about her. 'Did I?'

As he frowned she thought again how devastatingly attractive he was. He was like a dark angel fallen to earth. He made it so easy for her to make excuses for how natural it was that she should want him to notice her, to spend time with her, when logically she should tell him what she thought. He'd brought her here under false pretences, and now, like a pregnant mare, she was to be kept calm and quiet and safe until she was ready to foal. The offer to shadow him at work was just another of his sops to keep her quiet.

'You can shadow me, but not today,' he said, seeing the impatience she had tried so hard to keep off her face.

'When?' she prompted, standing in front of him when he moved to leave the room.

'When it's convenient for me.' He made an impatient gesture. 'I'm not sure exactly when. Talk to my secretary. She keeps my diary.'

'No.' He looked at her, speechless, but she wasn't going anywhere. Short of lifting her to one side, Luc had no option but to listen to what she had to say. 'I want to know what my job involves. The others have already started their working day. I want to start mine. And I don't want to be late when I report for duty. So, if not with you, then where should I be?'

He scanned the corridor over her head, as if he had other, more important places to be. 'Look, Emma…' His stare returned to fix on her face.

She was looking. She met his stare unblinkingly as Luc went on, 'I really don't have time for this—'

'Then make time.'

His head slowly lowered until his dark eyes were on a level with hers. 'I beg your pardon?' he said softly.

He could put all the menace he wanted into his tone. She hadn't come halfway around the world to sit twiddling her thumbs. 'I'm sure you heard me the first time.' She tried for pleasant. She even added a helpful smile. The familiar beat of arousal was back, but she blanked it, along with the mesmerising tone of his voice and Luc's dark stare. 'I was ignored in the meeting. No one explained how I could contribute to any of the projects under discussion, and as I don't have any files or papers to help me understand I'm relying on you to tell me.' She managed to keep calm, but inwardly she was fuming. Forget the lust and the compelling attraction. The way Luc was treating her was insulting.

'What's to understand, Emma? You have a beautiful apartment in the centre of Rio. You have a wardrobe of clothes a princess might envy.' He cast a disapproving look at the chain-store suit she had chosen to wear. 'Yet you put this rag on and insult me.'

'I chose this outfit because it belongs to me. I didn't set out to upset you. Shouldn't I be the one who is insulted to find a wardrobe of clothes appropriate for a billionaire's mistress, not only installed on your jet but here in what you term *my* apartment? I have no intention of becoming your mistress, Luc, so you can take those clothes out of *my* apartment and send them back.'

'Is this how it's going to be?' he demanded.

'I'm afraid it is.'

'You're not afraid of anything,' the man she had given herself to so joyfully remarked coldly. 'Why do you continue to deny yourself like this?'

'Because I can. Because I'm not the woman you seem to think I am. You accepted that I was upset in London because of my parents' death, and that I was behaving out of character, and yet now you seem to think that I will gladly fall into line because it suits you.'

'I'm trying to make you as happy as I can while you're here, while you seem to be doing everything in your power to put hurdles in my way.'

'Shall I spell it out to you?' she suggested. 'An apartment, however beautiful, together with wardrobes full of expensive clothes is only going to make me feel more awkward, not less. You brought me here under false pretences. You told me that I'd have a job—a proper job. I expected

to live in staff quarters and dress like my peers—
either in a uniform you provide or in my own
suitable clothes. I did not expect you to wheel me
out like some sort of pampered moll, and then
have to find my place amongst people who work
hard for a living. How the hell did you think that
was going to work out?'

'Have you quite finished?' he asked quietly.

'Yes.' She glanced at the door. 'You can leave
me to find my own way around. I can't think
what I could possibly learn by shadowing you.'

'Really?'

It was Luc's turn to block her way, and to her
amazement there was a smile hovering around
his mouth as if her rebellion had pleased, even
aroused him. She guessed it made the hunt all the
more entertaining for him. Too bad there wasn't
going to be a hunt. 'Yes, really,' she stressed, staring steadily into his mocking eyes.

'Are you suggesting I consider myself so far
above you in status—in every way possible—that
I don't think your small, feminine brain could

possibly accommodate the complexities of my complicated day?'

Oh, she hated it when he did this. He had turned her anger into the urge to smile back. 'I don't know what you think, Lucas, but I do know I'm going to make a success of this job, with or without your help.'

'With would be better, surely?' he murmured.

His expression had softened. There was humour in his eyes. Luc was at his most dangerous now. 'I'm afraid my defence mechanisms have just kicked into place, along with my urge to work,' she said, glancing at the door. 'So, if you'll excuse me?'

'And if I won't?'

His voice was a soft caress. Right now she would have preferred the whiplash of command. It was so much easier to counter. 'If I don't leave this room now, you will consider it a victory and think that gives you a licence to walk all over me in future. That isn't going to happen, Luc. This is a very serious situation for me, as it should be for you. But be assured that, whether you're my boss or not, I will give this job my very best.'

Now she could only wait.

It seemed a long few seconds before Luc finally stood aside and opened the door to let her go.

'What the hell do you think you're doing?'

'What the does it look as if I'm doing?' On her hands and knees, Emma glanced up at the storm cloud that was her boss, Lucas Marcelos, and then she carried on mopping up the spill.

'We have cleaners to do that,' he rapped. 'You are no longer a chambermaid, Emma.'

Her inner imp laughed. Luc's tone made it sound as if he'd waved the magic wand and she had been instantly transformed into a fairy princess—except that might be boring, stuck away in some stuffy palace. 'Excuse me?' Standing up, she straightened her skirt before confronting him. 'Is there some way this hotel could operate without its expert cleaning staff? Or are you suggesting I've somehow been elevated by our association into some new, rarefied sphere, where cleaning isn't necessary?'

'You know what I mean.' His jaw firmed.

'I don't think I do. There isn't a job in this hotel I wouldn't be prepared to do myself, but you haven't asked me to do anything. So what am I supposed to do? Am I supposed to sit upstairs in my apartment, reading magazines and painting my nails?'

'Now you're being ridiculous.'

'Am I?'

'You're overreacting. All I'm saying is that I don't expect to find you on your hands and knees, cleaning floors.'

'So there are jobs in this hotel you expect your staff to do that you wouldn't do yourself?'

'Of course I'm not saying that.'

'Then why can't I do this? What am I here for? What does everyone else think I'm here for? If it's to manage people, as you suggested back in Scotland, I have to understand every job, as well as the stresses the people doing that job have to face. And if a waiter has an accident with a tray because he's rushing from one room to the next, I not only have to help him, I have to understand how we can make the rota work more smoothly for him in the kitchen so he's not rushing around. Understand this, Luc. I am not going to stand by, watching something going wrong and doing nothing about it. And I'm not going to wait until you give me permission before I move.'

'Is that it?' he demanded mildly when she paused for breath.

'For now, but there are some very simple things that could be improved here. We need to talk.'

He huffed a laugh. 'You are so right about that.'

Luc's grip on her arm was non-negotiable. Dropping her used floor cloth on the cleaning trolley as he hurried her past it and on down the corridor, she flashed a reassuring smile at Karina, who was standing with a group of their colleagues in the lobby, watching this mini-drama play out with her mouth wide open.

Luc didn't let go of her until they had walked past his shocked secretary and into his office, where he closed the door and paused as if gathering his thoughts.

How best to deal with a rebellious woman who had no official duty to fulfil was probably uppermost in his mind, she thought, taking the chance to look around. Office was a term she'd use loosely in this instance. The master of this building's eyrie was a fabulous light and bright space with an incredible view over the city to the sea. It was surprisingly optimistic if you had to pin down the mood.

That would be because of the mega-money business deals conducted here, Emma reasoned. No expense had been spared. She didn't need to examine the art to know that every picture would be an original, or sweep her hand across the polished surface of Luc's desk to know that everything he owned was of the best—with the possible exception of Emma Fane, lately chambermaid with pride intact, now person of no account in Luc's eyes.

But he didn't own her. And she wasn't one of his possessions, Emma thought, spearing a glance at Luc. 'You've given me no proper job to do,' she said, getting in first when he swung around.

'I've told them to let you man the phones to-morrow,' he flashed back. 'You can answer a phone, can't you?'

'I can answer a phone politely, and so can a ten-year-old child. I'll put myself in the complaints department.'

'We don't have one.'

'That's what you think. There's always some-one who can't get a booking when they want one. Do you even know how popular this hotel is?'

'Of course I know.'

'Then you'll know we have regular guests who should have their loyalty recognised, and if the hotel happens to be full when they ring—'

'It's full most of the time,' he rapped, and with this came an impatient gesture.

'Exactly.' She faced him down. 'So either we should have a list of associate hotels to supply to loyal guests we can't accommodate, or we invest in some more real estate—create a super-haven, perhaps—'

'We? *We?*' Luc's face was a mask of fury. 'Who do the hell do you think you are?'

Emma slowly shook her head. 'I've been asking myself that question since I first got here.' Her jaw firmed as she lifted her chin to confront him. 'And let me make this clear. I'm not staying unless I can do a proper job. I'm not just filling in time until I have my baby, and to date you haven't seen me as anything other than an unfortunate encumbrance—the human element connected to the convenient womb for your child.'

Luc reeled back as if she'd slapped him. The expression on his face sent her thoughts into a tailspin. He had his shadows too, she remembered, and so far she didn't have a clue what they were. They had gone about things backwards when it came to knowing each other, and maybe she had gone in too hard just now, but she had to wake Luc up to the fact that she wasn't here to be a rich man's plaything.

'You're not just a convenient womb,' he said

at last, his face dark with thoughts she couldn't read. 'Just remember that I didn't even know you were pregnant, so you can't accuse me of using you as breeding stock, but now you are having a baby that you say is mine, you're my concern.'

'But not under your control.'

He looked at her, but didn't answer. He was taking a lot on trust, she conceded. She had told Luc he was the father of her baby, and he had chosen to believe her. She had no doubt that when the child was born there would be tests, but until then he was giving her the benefit of the doubt. Maybe Luc did care—about her and the baby—and caring was new to him. He certainly seemed concerned now, and he was surprised that she was so keen to get to work, but she had never been one to sit on the sidelines, looking on.

'New real estate,' he murmured, staring out of the window as he thought about her earlier remark.

If business was the way to touch him, the way to get this complex man to open up, then that was the key she would use for the sake of their child.

'You've got some good ideas,' Luc admitted, narrowing his eyes as he turned to look at her.

Condescending? Yes. But any step forward was progress in her book. She'd take it and mend his manners later. 'You've got to allow me to be useful to you, Luc.'

His eyes sparked briefly with inner thoughts, but then he turned cold again. 'I think I've done enough for you.'

'I don't know what you mean. You haven't done anything, except bring me here and put me under your nose so you can monitor everything I do.'

'And what's wrong with that?' he demanded. 'Why do you have to make things so difficult, Emma?'

'Why won't I fold and let you have your own way, don't you mean?' she countered. 'I'm not trying to be difficult. I'm just suggesting we try to find some common ground, but so far you haven't even made time to speak to me.'

'What am I doing now?' Luc demanded, his arms open wide.

'Occupying the same space isn't a guarantee

of communication between two people, Luc. It's just an opportunity.'

'So what are you suggesting?'

'You make room for me in your organisation. I'll do anything, but I must have a proper job.'

'I offered you a proper job. Did you think being my mistress would be easy?'

She laughed. She couldn't help herself. 'You are such a dinosaur. And my answer's still no.'

Angling his chin, Luc eased onto one hip as he surveyed her with a lazy stare. 'So you're not the same girl I had against a wall in London?'

For a moment she was too shocked to speak. 'You were as desperate for it too, I seem to recall.'

Luc's surprise at her counter-attack flashed across his face. He was so used to dominating everything and everyone around him that he took it as his right.

A tense silence resulted. She would not back down. And then a question came into her head. She had a baby to look forward to in her future, and the tragedy of her parents' wasted lives in her past, as well as hormones bombarding her, but what drove Lucas to behave so unreasonably? Her maternal instinct was in full flood, Emma accepted, hence the caring when otherwise she might have been inclined to walk out on him right now. 'I'm the mother of your baby,' she said steadily, 'and though neither of us can ever forget London, I would ask you to not to cheapen what we had.'

'What we had?' he said, frowning.

At least they were talking, she thought.

'You're right,' he said at last, nodding his head. 'We do have to sort this out.'

She was just breathing a sigh of relief when he added, 'I won't stand for you embarrassing me in front of my staff again.'

CHAPTER TEN

'EMBARRASS YOU?' Emma fired back as Luc closed the door, enclosing them both in the controlled atmosphere of his elegant boardroom. 'How do you think I felt when I arrived here? How do you think I felt walking into that meeting, where everyone knew me—or, at least, knew about me—but no one seemed to know what I was supposed to be doing at the meeting?'

'Of course they knew. I spoke to my secretary...' Luc's brow crinkled as if for once in his charmed life he had forgotten to mention that Emma would be attending the meeting.

'Either your secretary's incompetent or you forgot,' she said bluntly. 'Everyone was seated when I arrived. They weren't expecting me, and there was no place for me. You should try that on for embarrassment.'

'I was wrong in that instance,' Luc admitted tersely. 'So, what am I supposed to do about it?'

She firmed her jaw. 'Embarrassment I can recover from, but going forward I need something more. I need a reason to be here—a reason your staff can understand that doesn't involve my sharing your bed.'

'You're right,' Luc said thoughtfully, taking the wind from her sails. 'I left you stranded and I apologise for that, but there was a crisis to handle that couldn't wait. I could have given you clearer guidance.'

'You could have given me *some* guidance,' she argued quietly.

Luc's black eyes plumbed the depths of hers. 'Why the fuss, Emma? You're not as feeble as you make out. You're not feeble at all. You can handle embarrassment and any other situation that comes your way, so don't expect me to mollycoddle you while you're here.'

'I don't expect different treatment from the rest of your staff. I just expect the respect you show them. My intention is to do the best job possible for you. I can make my time here count, but you have to make that possible.' Luc was the gate-keeper. Without his say-so she would be a re-dundant cog in a very large wheel, with nothing to do other than to wait patiently for the birth of their child.

'Are you hungry?'

His change of tack was so swift she had to pause a moment. Luc's thoughts were always leaping ten steps ahead. So where were they now? She decided to play along and see where that took them. 'I'm expecting a baby. I'm al-ways hungry.'

'How about a late breakfast, and then we can chat through things?' he suggested.

'That will make me late for manning the phones, or whatever other work you decide I should do.'

'Not if we meet in the restaurant,' Luc argued. 'You can take a look around, eat, and then you can start work there immediately afterwards. Manning the phones can wait.'

'Work in the kitchens,' she murmured as she

thought about it. 'Better,' she agreed, remembering the waiters attending to room service and how they had to run about. Working in the kitchens would give her a proper chance to work out something more manageable for them.

'Have you eaten today?' Luc demanded.

Care for the brood mare, she thought, shaking her head with exasperation. 'I do have money with me, and there are cafés here. I'm not as helpless as you seem to think.'

'You're not helpless at all.' Luc's compelling stare narrowed on her face.

As always her body rejoiced, while she closed her mind to him. 'You don't need to worry. I am looking after myself.'

He seemed unconvinced as he led the way to their next destination.

It was early for lunch, and the corridor was deserted when they arrived outside the kitchens. Expecting Luc to open the door for her, she paused as he stepped in front of her. 'Aren't we going in?'

Luc's eyes were black and dangerous. 'Say please,' he taunted in a husky tone.

'I'll say something,' she promised briskly.

Her pulse was off the scale. They were close enough for her to see the flecks of gold in his eyes. They were breathing the same air, sharing the same space, two wills colliding; his fierce enough to bring him all the riches in the world, while hers was forged in steel out of sheer necessity. They were as unequal as two people could be in the material sense, but at their cores they were the same.

Gripping the handle, she swung the door wide. 'Shall we?' she prompted, stepping inside.

Luc was as good as his word. Emma was able to spend the rest of that week familiarising herself with the kitchens and the staff, though she rarely saw him. Whether Luc was keeping away from her on purpose, or whether he was just too busy visiting his hotels in other parts of the country, she had no idea.

His absence gave her some much-needed breathing space and time to reflect. Sometimes, when she was tired, she wondered what she was doing in Brazil—why she hadn't stayed in Scotland, and why she hadn't given herself more chance to mourn the deaths of her parents. She came up with the answer in the most unlikely circumstances, while she was doing the most monotonous task: cleaning out a deep fat fryer.

Mopping her brow with the back of her arm, she accepted that thinking about her parents always made her sad, because nothing had been resolved between them. She hadn't won their love and doubted now that that was possible. Sometimes hard truths took longer to accept, she thought, knowing the only certainty was that the harder she worked, the closer she came to her goal of providing a good life for her child. She might not have had the best role models for parenthood, but she loved her baby already, and her child was going to be the most wanted child on earth.

And now she stank. Cleaning out a deep fat fryer was the worst job she'd done so far. The smell of old oil pervaded everything, and by the time she had finished her hair was plastered to her face, and eau de oil was her least favourite scent. But she did have a great view of everything going on in the kitchen. Standing on the sidelines, taking notes, wouldn't have suited her. She didn't want people thinking she was afraid to get her hands dirty while everyone else was run off their feet. And there were benefits. She smiled as the chef offered her a titbit from his latest creation. 'Mmm, delicious.'

'You deserve it, Emma.'

She didn't know about that, but she'd learned a lot—and not just that the food at Luc's hotel was superb. If she could ease things in the future for her colleagues, she'd count it as a victory. And that was her primary concern—not where Luc was. So why was she fretting about him?

The answer came when she met Karina on her way out.

'You stink.' Standing well back, Karina faked an explosive coughing fit as she wafted the air with her manicured hand.

'I don't know whether to be flattered or to hit

you with a greasy cloth,' Emma admitted. 'But you're right. I do stink.'

'Like an old chip pan,' Karina confirmed. 'Didn't they give you an overall to wear?'

'I was covered from head to foot in designer plastic, but this exclusive cologne is what they call perma-stink oil.' With an appreciative hum she inhaled deeply and almost gagged.

'Better get yourself sorted out,' Karina advised. 'It's my birthday party tonight, and you're coming.'

Emma's face dropped. 'Oh, goodness. I'd forgotten! Joke,' she added, seeing the look on Karina's face. 'Of course I haven't forgotten. You wouldn't let me.'

'Quite right. Tired or not, you have to come. Someone has to keep my brother in line.'

'Your brother?'

'The Beast, otherwise known as Lucas? Don't look at me like that. I won't accept any of your lame excuses.'

Emma's head was spinning.

'You have to be there to stop him ordering me

about. This is the first time I've met a woman who can control him. Please don't spoil my fun now.'

'Lucas is your brother?' Emma mused. 'Of course he is,' she said faintly, suddenly seeing everything she'd missed in Karina's likeness to Lucas. 'But why didn't you mention it before?'

'I thought you knew. I thought Lucas would have told you.'

Emma hesitated. This was not the moment to admit that she didn't have that type of close relationship with Lucas.

'I know he's got it bad,' Karina added. 'I just can't understand why he hasn't thrown you to the floor and had his evil way with you. Judging by that scowl on his face, he hasn't.'

Emma forced a laugh. 'You don't seriously expect me to share trade secrets with his sister, do you?'

'Please, don't!' Karina exclaimed, pulling a face. 'But I will say this. You've certainly made an impression on him.'

She longed to tell Karina about the baby, but

as Luc's sister grabbed her arm to lead her away to chat about the party, she knew with a sinking heart that once again this wasn't the right time to raise the subject.

She had used a whole bottle of shampoo on her hair, and then had to choose something from her well-stocked dressing room to wear, as the suit she owned had winged its way to the hotel's dry-cleaning service, and her working day wasn't over yet. Housekeeping had asked if she could add the finishing touches to some recently renovated rooms before the first guests arrived. She just had time to fit that in before Karina's party. It was a job she was looking forward to. It didn't involve industrial cleaning methods and gave her the chance to evaluate what improvements could be made for guests, if any. Checking out her reflection in the mirror one last time, she grimaced. There was a lot to be said for the high-end designer's plain navy blue tailored suit teamed with a neat white blouse that Luc's team had chosen for her. It could be summed up in three words: Boring. Boring. Boring.

Calling Housekeeping, she asked if they had any spare uniforms handy.

Happy now she was dressed appropriately in one of the smart Marcelos-branded outfits, she headed out to complete her last task of the day before Karina's party.

A party. Hadn't she vowed to steer clear of parties?

Yes, but she couldn't let Karina down. And, as far as she knew, in spite of what Karina had said about controlling him, Luc wasn't back from his travels yet.

But wouldn't he make the effort to be there? Yes, he'd been away, but surely he'd be back for his sister's party?

If he was, so what? She was going for Karina's sake, not Luc's.

But now her heart was thundering. Part of her hoped he'd be there, while the other part of her had more sense.

* * *

'What are you working on today?'

'*What?*' Emma catapulted away from the bed she'd been straightening as Luc walked into the room. 'Don't touch me,' she yelped as he placed a reassuring hand on her arm.

'Steady,' he murmured.

'I'm not your horse.' Still recovering from the shock of seeing him, she gave him a glare, but she couldn't deny that she was pleased to see him.

'Forgive me,' he drawled, leaning back against the door. 'I didn't mean to surprise you.'

'So you just guessed I was up here in this room?'

A smile hovered around his mouth. Luc knew everything that happened in his hotel.

'How've you been while I've been away?'

Better. Calmer. A lot calmer than she felt now. 'I've been fine. Why shouldn't I be?' She glanced at the door, which he'd just closed behind him. 'How did you get in?'

Luc shrugged as he held up the master key. He was the master of all he surveyed—with one exception, who now straightened her spine to shoot him a hard look.

'What are you doing here?' he asked, frowning as he glanced around.

'Putting the finishing touches to this room.'

'Not bad,' he approved.

She held back on the curtsey. Casually dressed in black jeans and a black shirt with the sleeves rolled back, she guessed Lucas had been back at the hotel for some time and that he was fresh from the gym. The clock was creeping steadily towards evening, yet his hair was still damp from the shower...

Either that, or he's been in bed with someone.

'Are you all right?' he asked as she swayed.

'Never better,' she confirmed, sidestepping him neatly.

Had she really swayed at the thought of Luc in bed with someone else? Shutting out that ugly thought, she tried not to react in any way while the scent of his cologne, warmed and intensified by his body heat, invaded her senses like a drug.

Turning around to face him, she tilted her chin

to meet his keen stare, and was immediately dazzled by the expression in his eyes. The same potent combination of lust and humour was there, with, yes, a little caring in the mix. And even without that she'd missed him more than she'd realised.

That way lies heartache, Emma's inner guardian angel warned. Luc wanted sex, while she wanted so much more. 'I need to get on,' she said briskly, moving past him before the heat of his stare could do any more damage.

'You seem to be on edge,' Luc commented. 'What's wrong with you?'

'I don't want to be late for your sister's party.'

'Are you sure that's all? Is the baby okay?'

'The baby's fine. I would have said something—' She bit back the words, knowing they didn't have that type of close relationship. She would have to find a use for her hands or stop wringing them.

He stopped her at the door. 'So everything's going well with your pregnancy?'

'Yes.' The crazy part of her longed for Luc to

drag her into his arms, and say 'Good.' For him to whisper it against her hair as they shared the joy, but he didn't move and neither did she. Why would he? Why would she? She couldn't risk becoming reliant on anyone. She had to be strong enough to do this on her own. And Luc was going to make that difficult. There was only one way for him, and that was his way. It was up to her to find a compromise, though how she had no idea as yet. 'The doctor says everything is going to plan,' she said, feeling she ought to reassure him.

'Doctor?' Luc frowned.

'The hotel doctor is very helpful. I registered with him the morning after I arrived.'

'You have made yourself at home.'

'I've done what's necessary for my health and for the health of my baby.'

He eased away from the door. 'Our baby.'

Had Luc accepted their child? A little ray of hope lit inside her, but she didn't push it. 'The medical care you offer your staff is very good.'

'I'm glad you approve.'

'I would be a fool not to take advantage of it.'

'And no one would call you a fool, Emma.'

There was something in his voice that chilled her—something that said they had a long way to go before they could talk about trust—but while he'd been away it seemed that Luc had got used to the idea of a baby—his child, his heir—and that he was more enthusiastic about the whole idea. This was wonderful news for their child, but Luc would be more determined than ever to bring her under his control.

'I'd rather you didn't work,' he said, confirming her concerns.

'I have to work. And what I've been doing here isn't exactly hard.' She gestured around the beautiful room.

'It isn't slaving away in the kitchen,' Luc agreed, 'as my head chef assures me you are happy to do.'

She was chilled by the thought that he knew everything, but everyone in the hotel reported to Luc. 'Why am I here if not to work?'

'You should be resting.'

'You took me to the kitchens and set me to work.'

'Not to scrub and clean.'

'I won't pick and choose. I'll do whatever's necessary.'

'Will you?' Luc's voice and his manner had changed. He was warning her not to push him.

Tough. She wouldn't give in to him, Emma determined. Luc would enjoy her and then cast her aside as soon as she'd had the baby, if she gave him that chance, and she needed solid foundations for her child, which meant a good job going forward, so she wouldn't offend him. To get that good job, she'd need a glowing reference from Luc. She wouldn't do anything to compromise that.

'I'll see you at the party,' he said, looking at her with dark amusement as if he could read her mind.

'I'll be there,' she confirmed. 'I'm looking forward to it. You should have told me Karina was your sister.'

'I hear that you've become friends.' His dark eyes grew watchful. 'What do you talk about?' He opened the door for them.

She shrugged. 'This and that.'

'Have you told my sister about the baby?'

'No, and tonight is Karina's night, so I won't be mentioning it.'

Luc remained silent as he waited for her to go ahead of him.

'Is there something else?' She paused, close enough to feel his heat warming her.

'You haven't mentioned missing me.'

Tingles shimmered down her spine.

'No, that's right, I haven't.' With a last quick glance in his direction, she walked away.

CHAPTER ELEVEN

THE USUAL CHAOS REIGNED. This was his sister's annual party madness. He had detailed a squad of security guards to keep an eye on things, but he patrolled the vast marquee, because control was important to him. Control was vital.

He was looking for one person, and she had not arrived. The noise was ferocious. Even when he left the tent and checked outside, the noise inside easily crested the sound of the surf. This year's celebration was being held on the beach, far away from the hotel and the sensibilities of his guests. He'd had a vast marquee erected on a piece of land he owned. The suggestion Emma had made about new real estate was ticking away in the back of his mind. He could just as easily build an annex to the hotel here.

Emma was strong on ideas—strong in many

ways. For once in his life he regretted that past experiences had made him the man he was and long-term relationships were off his radar. Life had taught him to be a realist. He'd move on, and so would she.

His mouth tugged a little as he turned back to face this year's extravaganza. His sister was an events organiser second to none, which was why he'd hired her. His company was too fast-moving, too successful, to allow for nepotism. Karina's ideas were always off the wall, which was what made her stand out in the industry.

This year's theme was the Arabian Nights, which meant the colossal tent was decked out in every exotic shade under the sun. The walls were composed of billowing silk sheets in a variety of jewel colours, while countless torches lit the scene. There were bare-chested waiters offering guests drinks, and bonfires on the beach where couples or groups could retire to cook their own food if they felt the need to escape the frenzy of the party for a while. The roof of the marquee was pleated and gathered into a small turret enclosed by a golden crown, on top of which flew a flag embellished with the letters K.M.

It was extravagant, but he would do anything for the sister who was lucky to be alive. Never a day passed when he didn't remember that he had put her in mortal danger.

And with that thought making him edgy, he searched again for Emma. Where was she? And where was his sister? He didn't know how he felt about the two of them being in cahoots, but he did know that Karina should be here to greet her guests.

What would Emma be wearing tonight? He'd seen that flash of fire in her eyes, enough to remind him of the wild woman he'd bedded in London. He doubted Emma would ever lose that side of her completely—he hoped she wouldn't. He straightened up as he saw her coming down the path. As he had suspected she would be, Emma was arm in arm with his sister. Her laughter reached him first, and then her jade-green gaze settled on his. Tilting her chin at the defiant angle he was becoming used to, she walked straight past him across the sand. The chiffon robe she was wearing was the same colour as her eyes and floated behind her as she walked. Her feet were bare, except for dainty flat, strappy sandals, and she'd painted her toenails shell pink. They gleamed iridescently in the moonlight, while her skin looked paler than usual, highlighting the differences between them.

He felt like a barbarian lusting after a nymph. It was an arousing thought. In a totally frivolous touch Emma had secured a band of paste emeralds around her brow in an attempt to contain her long red hair. Defying these efforts, it floated around her shoulders like a fiery cloak. He had to have her tonight or he'd go mad.

'But we're just going to dance,' his sister protested, when he came to stand between them.

'You should greet your guests,' he told Karina. 'Shall we?' he said to Emma. Without waiting for her answer, he linked arms with her and led her away.

'That was high-handed.' Emma arched a brow as she stared up at him.

She didn't attempt to move away, he noted.

'You are impossible, Lucas,' she said, using his full name to show her disapproval. 'You think you can push everyone around, even your own sister, but don't expect me to come running when you snap your fingers.'

He had halted at the edge of the surf and moved in front of her. Putting his hands on her arms, he held her where he could look into her eyes. 'I expect you to come to me of your own accord.' Emma snatched a breath as he added, 'Don't fight me, Emma. Don't fight this…'

Her hands flew up to press flat against his chest. Brushing them away, he dipped his head and lightly kissed her.

'Stop it,' she warned.

'You'd rather go back to my sister?'

'I'd rather kiss you.' Her eyes widened as if the words her left her lips without making contact with her brain. 'I should go back,' she said quickly. 'Karina will be missing me.'

He smiled faintly. 'Karina will have forgotten both of us by now.'

Emma's stare flashed to the marquee where they could both see Karina surrounded by a circle of friends.

Emma turned back to look at him. 'Perhaps you're right.'

'I know I'm right.'

He led her away into the shadows. He knew this beach like the back of his hand. He'd come here as a boy and had explored every inch of it. He knew where to stop, to sit, to lie, and even where to make love. He'd lost his virginity here to an older woman, back in the days when he had still believed that love was real. The relentless thrust and pound of the waves on the shoreline was the soundtrack to his life.

'I won't break my own rules,' Emma told him, hanging back.

'What rules are we talking about?' Dipping down, he rolled his jeans up to his knees so he could thrash his way through the surf.

'My rules,' she yelled back at him above the crash of the surf. 'No parties. No Luc. No sex.'

'Rules are made to be broken.' Emma had

kicked off her sandals, and was bundling her dress up so she could do the same, he noticed as he laughed.

'Not mine,' she said, swishing through the shallows until she arrived at his side. 'And why should I break them?' Her eyes turned serious as she looked at him. 'You never make yourself vulnerable or talk about your past. You keep the real Luc hidden away. You never show anything of yourself—what you're feeling, your thoughts about the future, or the past. Or if you do, you don't share those thoughts with me. So tell me, why should I break my rule, Lucas?'

'Because you can?'

She laughed and shook her head as she stared out to sea. 'No means no.'

Turning to do the same, he inhaled deeply. The refreshing scent of ozone mingling with the aroma of a woman he was beginning to find irreplaceable was a heady combination. He enjoyed it for quite a while before turning to her. 'No dancing?'

'No dancing wildly,' she said, reminding them

both of London, when dancing with abandon had attracted the attention of her boss and had led to places neither of them had expected.

'A sedate waltz should be safe,' he suggested.

'In Brazil?' She flashed him a look that was pure wild Emma.

It hit his senses like a wrecking ball. What chance did he have when the music gliding towards them from the marquee was so sexy and sinuous? 'A rumba,' he murmured: sex in dance form. The rumba was the dance of love, the dance of seduction. It was a dance that gave him the perfect excuse to draw Emma close. In the first light-hearted moment they had ever shared they danced barefoot in the sand.

One dance couldn't hurt, Emma told herself as she closed her eyes and melted into Luc's arms. She didn't want anyone to see them, especially not Karina, before she had told Luc's sister about the baby. She wanted everything above board with Karina. She'd grown fond of Luc's sister and wanted to break the news to her gently. She hated the deception that fate seemed be to thrusting on her time after time.

And she was deceiving herself now if she thought this dance could end in a gentle stroll back to the marquee, but she couldn't snap herself out of the trance that dancing with Luc had brought on. They moved together so easily and he was so achingly familiar…

And dangerously unknown.

Emma frowned. What did she know about Lucas Marcelos? Barely anything. What did anyone know? The public only knew what Luc allowed them to know. He edited every bit of information about himself stringently. Which suggested to her that there was a lot he kept hidden.

She shivered involuntarily with pleasure as he feathered touches down her arm. It was so easy for Luc to make her forget everything…everything except him and the moment.

Winding a lock of her hair around his hand, he drew her head back and kissed her neck. It was such an intimate thing to do. It was a reminder of all the intimacy they had shared. Resting her hands on Luc's shoulders, she stared into his eyes. The one thing they hadn't shared before was peace like this. They had only known fire and passion, chaos and noise, surprises and shock, but this sinuous dance was a time for just feeling close. Drawing closer was as inevitable as the sea breeze caressing her overheated skin. It tempted her to believe that Luc had learned to feel, and she wondered if the baby had brought that change about.

She didn't resist when he led her away towards the palm-fringed rear of the beach, where the undergrowth rustled in the ocean breeze. A comfortable hollow offered privacy and a bed with a moonlit, star-strewn canopy. Stretching his length alongside her, Luc brought her into his arms and kissed her in the way she had dreamed about since they'd first met. Her body and her heart yearned for him and she was already whimpering with need long before his touch on her body became firmer and more demanding.

Pressing against him, she writhed to increase the contact between them. A shaking cry escaped her when Luc smoothed his hand over the swell of her buttocks. His touch transferred to everywhere that had missed him, like a promise she ached for him to fulfil. Her long, filmy skirt proved no barrier at all. She may as well have been naked—a thought that had almost certainly crossed Luc's mind. He smoothed the skirt back and she adjusted her position. Her lace thong was soon discarded. She was already throbbing with pleasure when he moved between her thighs. Reaching beneath her, he cupped her buttocks to bring her up to him, while with the other hand he brought her wrists above her head. She smiled against his mouth. This was exactly what she wanted.

Breath hitched in her throat as Luc teased her with the tip of his arousal. It was a promise of pleasure that made her pulse race. Over and over he went, back and forth, never quite giving her what she wanted, but Luc had never been in a rush.

Tonight she was in a rush, and arced up to claim him. 'Now,' she instructed, holding him captive with her inner muscles.

The pace of Luc's breathing shot up and his
eyes turned black with passion. Holding her
stare so she couldn't look away, he thrust slowly
into her, and then just as slowly withdrew. Another firm thrust to the hilt...one more roll of
his hips, and she was screaming his name as he
murmured, 'Now...'

She moved convulsively, lost in pleasure, for
the longest time, with Luc holding her in place.
It was too much—too good—and she couldn't
come down. She didn't want to come down. She
wanted to remain suspended in Luc's erotic net
for ever, moaning rhythmically as each succes-
sive pleasure wave rolled over her and carried
her to a new, higher level of sensation.

'Open your legs as wide as you can,' he instructed. 'Think of that one place and what I'm
doing to you.'

It seemed impossible that mere words could
make her pleasure grow, but Luc knew everything about her body and her responses to his instructions. She lost control again before he had
finished speaking.

'Greedy,' he chastised her, smiling against her mouth.

'Very greedy,' she confirmed happily when it was finally possible to speak.

They kissed, they touched, and they shared whispered confidences. They made love for what seemed like hours. And they did make love. It wasn't just sex, Emma reassured herself as Luc kissed her again. Even his kisses had changed. Everything he did now was tender and gentle, deeper and more meaningful, as if he really did care for her. The thought that they might have a future together dazzled her like a golden chalice just out of reach. To think of a future together with their child—

No, No! She couldn't—she mustn't allow herself to think like that. She had to remain strong. She had to go forward into the future self-reliant and independent, not looking to Luc and hoping he would care for her, or look at her a certain way, though right now she had never felt closer to another human being in her life.

'Okay?' he murmured, carefully withdrawing.

'Okay,' she confirmed, as he rolled onto his side so they were face to face.

Everything about tonight was okay—more than okay, it was magical. Making love to Luc beneath a canopy of stars was like every one of her dreams coming true. She could have lain here kissing him for the rest of the night. She could have lain here with her legs wrapped about his powerful thighs for ever.

'What?' he demanded softly, when she stirred.

'You,' she said, looking at him. She held his stare, wondering if at last she'd found the key to unlocking Luc's inner self. She was so sure he was starting to trust her that she dared to hope they could go forward together now. No sooner had the thought lodged in her mind than Luc moved away and sprang up. She felt instantly bereft, robbed of more than just his warmth. His focus had left her too, she saw.

Making quick work of fastening his jeans, he stared down at her. 'Well, I'm glad I make you smile.'

'I'm glad you've changed,' she said, clinging

to those precious times they'd just shared, even though, deep down, she suspected they were already consigned to the past as far as Luc was concerned.

'Changed?' He frowned as he secured his belt. 'Changed into what?'

'From arrogant and distant, to loving and…'

When was she going to stop this? When was she going to wake up and realise that Luc didn't share the hopeless romanticism in her psyche?

Also, she was hormonal. And right now she was riding a wave of euphoria that came after making love, while Luc had had sex with her and his head was perfectly clear.

'Oh, I don't know…'

'You said loving?' he prompted with a frown.

He'd pick up that one careless word. 'Loving as in…not so controlling?' she suggested, trying to make light of what had been a dangerously careless remark.

As Luc helped her to her feet, she had to remind herself that he didn't do love. But she did. More fool her.

She brushed herself down while Luc stared back at the lights of the party. It was time to go.

'What's wrong?' he said when she hesitated.

'Nothing.' And this was the man she had briefly thought so tender and caring? Not even a kiss or a touch to reassure her now. She had a lot to learn about the complex man that was Lucas Marcelos, but doubted she would ever get that chance—

'Ready?' she said brightly, starting back to the marquee.

CHAPTER TWELVE

LUC'S SMILE MADE her wary. Step one had been achieved as far as he was concerned. Emma was in Brazil. Step two had also been a success. He'd had her. Why would he have any reason to suppose she'd want to go anywhere until he'd done with her? Sex was sensational between them. Luc was a tireless lover who enjoyed bringing her pleasure. What woman wouldn't want to be with a man like that?

Just don't go looking for Luc's heart, because you'll be looking for a long time.

She knew that. Sex was essentially a sport for Luc. He used it to exert control over her, or so he thought. Setting her sights on her goal, which was the marquee and uncomplicated fun with Luc's sister, she barred herself from looking back at him.

He caught up with her, and standing in front of her he stopped her going anywhere. 'Excuse me, please. I'm already late for the party.'

'Late?' He frowned.

'Okay. Very late. Will you please let me pass?'

'You're not just very late,' he said, humour lighting up his eyes, 'Your hair's a mess, your legs are covered in sand.' He shrugged as he plucked some foliage from her hair. 'And, if I'm not mistaken,' he said, leaning close, 'you're also mad at me. Now, why can that be?'

Could it be because you're so cold-hearted?

Reaching out, Luc took his fingertips on a feathery trail down her face to her lips where his fingertip lingered. 'Don't be angry, Emma. We'll go in to the party together. I don't think there are many secrets at the hotel,' he added, confirming her own thoughts on that subject. 'You're in the apartment next to mine, waiting to give birth to my child. No one knows you're pregnant yet, but you won't be able to hide it for very much longer.'

'Even so, my independence is vital to me.'

'Independence *was* vital to you before the baby

came along.' Luc's voice had gained an edge. 'But now you have other concerns, I would have thought.'

'I do have other concerns.' His implication that she was being selfish made her mad. 'You really will stop at nothing. And I'll say it one more time. I will not become your mistress.'

Luc responded with a dismissive gesture. 'That's fine by me. Pay your own way. Work all you want to. In fact, I insist you work—just not the hours you worked in Scotland. You're too valuable an asset, as far as my company is concerned, for me to allow your talents to go to waste. But the child will be supported by both of us.'

Luc's eyes had turned stony. His expression scared her. 'How will that work?'

'I'll plug any gaps you leave.' His eyes drilled into hers as if hunting for signs of weakness.

He'd find none, she determined, though the gaps Luc referred to would be huge compared to his thick bankroll. She couldn't hope to compete with the type of life he seemed determined to give his child.

'For once in your life agree, and be thankful, Emma.'

He hadn't really changed at all. 'Thankful?' she said quietly, feeling that all their closeness had been destroyed. 'You make me feel as if I come to you like a beggar—and that what I can provide will never be enough for our child.'

'I'm just stating facts.' Luc's shoulders lifted in a careless shrug. 'I'm saying I can give more.'

'I can support my child,' she said firmly. 'And I'll do that with or without your help—'

'You will do what is right,' Luc said over her. 'This isn't about you, Emma, this is about my child.'

His child. His control. His world.

She had never felt more vulnerable or alone.

Which was all the reason to gather her forces and fight. She wasn't alone. She had a baby to protect. 'If you're suggesting that by doing as you say, I'll somehow earn more treats for my child, I think that's despicable, and we're going to have some real problems down the line. I'm going into the party now. I think we need space—'

'Don't play games with me, Emma.' She gasped as Luc yanked her close. 'This is too important. You can't walk away from me.'

'And you can't walk away from this problem, which will remain until you learn to let go,' she shot back. 'We're in this together—equal partners, whether you like it or not. Now, get off me,' she warned, angrily shaking herself free.

'We're well matched,' Luc commented, not in the least bit fazed.

'You wish,' she said quietly, stalking off.

Her breath shattered into pieces as Luc brought her back into his arms and silenced her with a kiss. He held her so she couldn't escape his heat and force, and for a moment she wanted to yield. Thankfully, this time common sense kicked in before she did. 'No, Luc. We have to talk. And before we do that, I need space from you.'

'But I don't need space from you,' he murmured, smiling his way into her heart. She groaned as he rolled his hips and then made things worse, bending again at the knees and straightening up slowly, rubbing her where she was still so sensitive. He kept up the pressure until her body screamed for him, and wanting Luc was like a madness driving her closer to the brink.

'You don't want to go anywhere,' he said quietly.

She swallowed convulsively, knowing he was right. But she was equally certain she should say, *No! I can do without you.* She should pull away from him and go back to the party, but she couldn't…she didn't want to. She wanted Luc.

'You want me to have you here where anyone might see or hear,' he said, seducing her with his wickedness. 'You want to take that risk that someone could leave the party and head towards the beach, instead of the road—walk right past us while I'm pleasuring you. In fact, the prospect excites you.'

'Luc, stop this,' she begged. 'We can't—'

'But we are,' he said. 'You don't want me to stop.'

'But we could be discovered.'

He smiled as he freed himself. 'That doesn't

bother you. You've got other things on your mind right now, such as me attending very thoroughly to your needs.'

She whimpered in helpless agreement as he cupped her. And then his hand began to work, rhythmically and persuasively, until she couldn't have stopped him had she tried. Her body had taken over her mind and her actions, and a cry of need flew from her throat. Nothing else mattered but this.

'I was right, wasn't I?' Luc said, smiling against her mouth. 'I'm going to do everything,' he said, 'and you don't even have to move.'

That was one instruction she couldn't follow. She was already scrambling up him when Luc lifted her. She couldn't wait. She couldn't stand for his teasing or tormenting her, or for foreplay of any kind. She had to have him now... and cried out with satisfaction when Luc's first stroke drove deep. He filled her completely. He stretched her beyond imagining. The shock was sensational—the pleasure even better. She lost control immediately and bucked against him, out of her mind with triumph and relief, and very soon after that a craven hunger for more.

'Wait,' he commanded, his voice a soft, husky drawl. 'You're too greedy by far. You're going too fast.'

'No,' she growled, collapsing against him.

'Try to think of something else,' he suggested.

'How am I supposed to do that?' she gasped out.

'Do it,' Luc commanded.

She dragged deeply on his warm, clean scent, revelling in everything about him, knowing that if she did as Luc said the pleasure would be stronger and would last even longer. But there came a point where she couldn't wait and arching towards him she took him deep, moving fiercely and fast, relishing the feast of sensation—wailing as she crashed over the cliff. She clung to him furiously as he made sure she was done.

Luc rested inside her, smoothing her hair with long, calming strokes, and when she was calm again he withdrew slowly and with infinite care.

But he was only teasing her and plunged deep

again. The shock was glorious. The pleasure was intense. She responded immediately, coming apart in his arms as he pressed deep and rolled his hips. 'More!' She laughed. 'Give me more,' she begged him, as if they hadn't done this over and over in the sand.

She would never get enough of him, Emma realised as to her relief Luc began to move.

He gave her what she needed in a series of firm, deep strokes. And then repeated the technique he had used before, withdrawing slowly and thrusting firmly, driving her further and further up the thick smooth strut of the marquee. She dug her fingertips into the muscles on his shoulders, her arms almost straight he'd pushed her so high. Throwing her head back, she gasped noisily as she silently sang the praises of this big, powerful man.

'Again?' he suggested when she quietened.

'Are you asking permission?'

Luc's answer was to drive into her and pleasure them both this time with fast, hard strokes.

'Yes!' she screamed, loving the sensation even more when he lost control with her.

'That has never happened to me before,' he admitted when they had both recovered. 'I was so angry with you—'

'And me with you,' she agreed.

'How am I keep supposed to keep a rein on myself now?'

She stared into his eyes, uncertain whether Luc was joking or not. 'Maybe you're not,' she said as he held her close. She pressed her face against his chest. Their heartbeats were equally rapid, but did Luc feel as she did inside? If there was some potion she could take to render her immune to Luc, she'd take it so she could be as cool as he was, but right now she had never felt so close to another human being in her life, and that felt so good she wanted to shout it to the world, not keep it hidden deep inside.

Outrageously good sex and a shared sense of humour, along with a certain amount of caring, was a tender shoot on which to build a relationship.

But it was a start, Emma told herself firmly as she straightened her clothes.

I love you, you impossible man, was what she wanted to say to him, but of course she didn't. It was too soon. Luc might laugh—would laugh, she corrected herself. The time might never come, and she had to accept that. From what she could tell, Luc had spent his entire adult life keeping people at bay, and one passionate encounter on a beach wasn't going to change that.

He linked fingers with her and led her through the entrance of the marquee. He didn't care who saw them. Emma had made him happy. She had made him feel good about himself for the first time in a long time.

'You can't refuse to be my mistress now.'

'I'm sorry?' She stopped dead and looked up at him. 'So you think that what just happened means you can drink your fill of me and then get rid of me? No,' she said levelly. 'Where becoming your mistress is concerned, nothing has changed.'

'Why?' Bringing his face close, Luc brushed her lips with his.

'Why am I the only woman on earth to refuse you? I don't know,' Emma admitted, pulling back. 'I just know that what you're offering is never going to be enough for me. However you dress it up, you're asking me to forfeit my freedom in return for financial gain.'

'So you don't feel anything for me?'

'Of course I feel something for you—too much,' she admitted. 'But nothing's changed because of tonight. I won't live with you. And I won't become your mistress. I should never have agreed to stay in that fabulous apartment to begin with. I should have had enough wit to demand accommodation in your staff quarters from the start. Then we wouldn't be having this conversation.'

Luc stared down at her indulgently. 'You do know this is hormones talking?'

'No, Luc.' Emma shook her head. 'This is me talking. We're back to where we started, so I'm telling you all over again that I won't be controlled.'

'That's not what I'm trying to do.'

'So what are you proposing?'

Not marriage, he thought as Emma turned away. He'd been down that dark alley once before and had no intention of repeating his mistake.

When he didn't answer, she shook her head in despair at him.

'You're a riddle, Emma,' he admitted. 'You're the most passionate woman I've ever known, but you say I'm controlled? What about you?'

'I don't want to hear about your other women,' she told him firmly. 'I certainly don't want to be compared to them.'

He could feel her pulling away in spirit, and they were already standing six feet apart. Emma glanced back towards the hotel, rather than towards the party, where they might have prolonged their evening. Losing her was unthinkable, he realised suddenly. He couldn't allow it to happen. He was confident he could pull this back. It wasn't the first time in his life he had faced an apparently insurmountable problem and triumphed. He had turned the scorn of the father he could never hope to impress into a positive that had driven him to succeed. Would he let Emma get the better of him?

'Goodnight, Lucas.'

Goodnight? He stood in silent disbelief as he watched her go. She was leaving him? She was walking away?

She didn't look back.

CHAPTER THIRTEEN

KARINA RAN UP to him and put a hand on his arm. 'Don't,' she cautioned. 'Don't go after her yet, Luc. Give her time.'

'Time for what?' He was in no mood to discuss Emma with his sister.

'You know why I'm saying this,' Karina insisted.

'Do I?'

'You don't want to rehash the past—I know that, but sometimes it has to be faced. You have to tell her, Luc. You can't keep avoiding the subject.'

He shook his head—the head he badly needed to get together. So much had happened in so short a time, the events he had been ignoring were back. All the old anger, the hurt, the sense of betrayal... Karina was right. He had to come to terms with it before he could move on. But not here where the noise from the party was deafening—or even in the hotel, where the demands of his work were ceaseless and would cause constant interruptions to his thought processes. There was only one place on earth where he could unspool the tangle and rewind.

'Please,' Karina was saying to him, hanging on to his arm as she stared up into his face. 'Don't let Emma go. Can't you see what you stand to lose? Emma's changed you for the better, and I'd rather see you like this—all beat up inside—than not feeling at all. Give love a chance, Luc.'

'Love?' he exclaimed with an incredulous laugh. 'I think you're overstating the case.'

'Am I?' his sister demanded. 'Yes, Lucas. Love. I'm not frightened of the word. Why are you? Just because you've been hurt once doesn't mean you'll be hurt again. Give yourself a chance, Luc. This could be your one chance to be happy again.'

He laughed bitterly, knowing it was easier to let the ice grow back around his heart.

'Everyone has secrets,' Karina persisted. 'It's who you choose to share them with that counts.'

'Thanks for the counsel, little sister. There are more secrets than you know.'

'There you go again,' she said. 'You're a patronising, arrogant pain in the butt—who means well, but who goes about things all the wrong way. You don't have to take the world on your shoulders. Emma and I can do that for ourselves.'

'I doubt it,' he murmured, narrowing his eyes as he stared in the direction Emma had gone. She had disappeared out of sight. He was itching to chase after her. Karina might have made sense. Both he and Emma needed space, but Emma's safety was his paramount concern now. 'I'm going after her.'

'Of course you are,' Karina told him with a smile in her voice.

He caught up with Emma running along the beach. She was barefoot, holding her sandals in one hand and her skirt in the other so she could run faster. The wind had caught hold of her hair and was tossing it about. He wanted to stand

and watch her but he couldn't let her carry on. 'Emma! Wait!'

Whipping her head around, she shouted back at him, 'Go away, Luc. This is over. I'm leaving. I never want to see you again.'

She was running away from him along a strip of ivory sugar sand, with the moonlight in her hair and the surf pounding at her feet. He raced along the sand to join her, and was with her in seconds. 'This has nothing to do with control,' he shouted against the wind, raising his hands in mock surrender when she looked at him. 'Do you know how dangerous this is? Running along the beach at night on your own—and in your condition?'

'Pregnancy isn't a threat to my health, Luc.'

'But an attack on a woman on her own at night is a threat,' he insisted, catching her close. 'You must never do this again. Do you understand me?'

She didn't fight him this time. In some calm part of her she knew he was talking sense. 'No, Luc, no,' she said softly. 'Don't say anything. I should never have come to Brazil. I should have told you about the baby when we were in Scotland, and I should have stayed there. But I had to be stubborn and come here, and now I've complicated everything.'

'When is life ever straightforward?' He brushed a wayward strand of hair from her face.

'It's not straightforward tonight,' she agreed. 'Tonight is so complicated that I need to take a step back, but if you want to see me safely to the hotel...'

'Of course I will.'

'I was silly to run off. You were right about the hormones.' She shook her head. 'They rule me.'

'I know.' He paused before suggesting, 'What if there were no conditions to your staying?'

She shrugged. 'I'd stay?'

'Seriously?'

'But only if I can move into the staff quarters, and only if you let me stand or fall by my own merit.'

Everything she asked for was contrary to his nature, but he couldn't *deal* with Emma as he

dealt with everything else in life. He would have
to learn to compromise. They both would. 'We'll
have to talk this through.'

'No surrender on the staff accommodation,'
she warned him.

Staying close but not touching was the most
extreme torture known to man, but he did as
he had promised and took Emma straight back
to the hotel. They walked in silence the entire
way, and by the time they arrived in the lobby
something significant had changed. Even though
they hadn't spoken, it was as if a wall had come
down.

'Thanks for giving me the space I asked for,'
she murmured as they waited for the elevator.

He stood back as the steel doors slid open.
'Goodnight, Emma. I'll have someone sort out
your accommodation.'

'Thank you.'

He stood for a moment staring at polished steel
as her face disappeared behind the sliding doors,
and then, decision made, he turned on his heels
and walked away.

* * *

She had asked Luc to back off and give her space. She hadn't expected him to take her quite so literally, Emma reflected, chewing on her lip as she headed out of her new and very comfortable room in the staff quarters. They hadn't spoken to each other since Karina's party and that was days ago. She had lain awake at night since then wondering where he was, and had asked different members of staff, only to be told that Senhor Marcelos was away on one of his trips. She didn't like to ask Karina. She had too much to tell her before that, and as Karina had been busy the old story of the right moment to talk about the baby had never come.

She found Karina sitting at their usual table in the staff canteen. She looked up as Emma approached.

'You look as if you haven't slept. Frustration keeping you awake?'

Ignoring this, Emma pulled a concerned face as she sank down onto the seat next to her friend.

'Sat up all night worrying about the lack of hot water in my bathroom, if you must know.'

'As diversionary tactics go, that was lame,' Karina remarked. 'Hot water?' she repeated suspiciously, scooping up another mouthful of aromatic sauce. 'Really?'

'Yes. Really. The shower in my room,' Emma explained, blinking owlishly as she forced out the story. 'There's something wrong with it. It made me think it might be worth completing a snagging list on every apartment in the staff quarters, so that's what I've done.'

'Of course you have,' Karina commented drily, getting back to her food.

'The plumber's coming round today to check them all out.'

'That's not the kind of plumbing I had in mind,' Karina murmured, shooting a look at Emma.

'Oh.'

'Exactly. Oh,' Karina echoed. 'I know about you and my brother, so no use pretending. Did you really think I wouldn't notice you were missing from the party? For *ever*?' she emphasised, rolling her eyes. 'Or that when you left, Luc chased after you?' she added when Emma started to protest.

'That was nothing.' She brushed this off with a casual gesture. 'Luc saw me safely back to the hotel, and that was it.'

Karina hummed as if she didn't believe a word of it. 'Did he say anything when he caught up with you?'

'Like what?'

Karina lips pressed down as if she wasn't quite sure whether to say something or not.

'Well?' Emma pressed.

'So…' Clearly determined to change the subject, Karina swung around to pin her with a stare. 'Let's get back to that night. If you say there's nothing between you and my brother, what about earlier when you arrived at the party looking flushed and excited with a dusting of sand and grass in your hair? Was that nothing too?'

'That was—'

'All right—not sure I want to know,' Karina interrupted. 'Anything more than a confession about a peck on the cheek and you won't need a sauce for your spaghetti.'

'Nice.'

'Stating facts. What's going on between you two? And, more importantly, what's gone wrong? That's what I want to know. It was clearly getting serious and now it's not.'

'How do you know all this?' Emma sat back in her chair, bemused.

'I know because when my brother takes off like this, it can only mean one thing. He's got something on his mind and needs to get away. He's been gone for over a week now, so it must be serious. And you very carefully haven't asked me where he's gone. So I'm obviously suspicious. And then there's you,' Karina added. 'I only have to look in your eyes to know there's something wrong with you. And whatever it is, you've got to get it sorted—both of you. What can be so bad that you can't talk about it face to face?'

Upsetting Karina was the last thing Emma wanted. 'I'm afraid it's a lot more than a disagreement,' she admitted.

'Well, tell me. Come on. What's the big news?'

'I'm having Luc's baby,' Emma blurted. She braced herself for Karina's response. Karina's hand had flown to her mouth and her face had paled with shock, but if there was one thing Emma had learned, it was that waiting for the right moment didn't work. Thankfully, Karina recovered quickly, and leaping out of her seat, she exclaimed, 'But that's wonderful!'

Sending plate and pasta dishes flying everywhere, she hugged Emma across the table. 'I can't believe you look so worried about it.'

'It's not that easy.'

'What's easy?' Karina exclaimed with a shrug, sitting down. 'Is there anything I can help you with?'

'The problem is Lucas.'

'Ah. That might be difficult.'

'It's not him exactly…' Emma hesitated. 'It isn't easy to share this with his sister—'

'Give it a try,' Karina advised. 'I'm your friend. Who better to confide in?'

'I just don't know how to say this in a less hurt-
ful way,' Emma admitted.

'Luc is controlling? Does that help?'

The expression on Karina's face made it hard
not to laugh. 'He wants to control everything,'
Emma admitted. 'He wants to control me at work,
when I'm away from work, my pregnancy, the
baby, me—'

'I know Luc can be difficult,' Karina interrupted, 'but there's a very good reason for it.'

'Can't you tell me what it is?'

Karina bit her lip and shook her head, as if
she'd already said too much. 'It's not for me to
tell you. You'll have to ask Luc.'

'That might be difficult when I don't even
know where he is. We didn't part on the best of
terms. I stalked off.'

'You behaved like every other couple in love?'
Karina suggested.

'We're not in love.'

'Aren't you?'

'I told him I needed space, and he took me at
my word.'

'Luc hasn't gone for ever. I've never seen him happier than he is with you. You have to give him a second chance, Emma. Speak to him, and then you'll understand why Luc is the way he is.'

Emma was silent as she considered this. 'You'd better tell me where he is.'

'He's at the ranch where we spent summers growing up. We sold the main family house in Rio because of memories we prefer to forget, but we kept the ranch house, the land and the old cabin as a reminder of our holidays there. We just couldn't bring ourselves to lose contact with the people who worked the ranch. They were like family. They still are. Luc bought the adjoining fazenda so he can ride out to the cabin like before.'

'How far away is it?' Emma's brain was racing.

'It's a couple of hours to fly to the ranch, and then another couple of hours to ride out to the cabin. You're not thinking of going there on your own, are you? Can you even ride? The cabin's in the middle of nowhere, and you're pregnant.'

'Yes. But I'm not sick, and I'm not helpless.

Exercise for pregnant women is actively encouraged, and this is something I've got to do. Tell me about the cabin,' Emma insisted, in an attempt to distract her friend.

'It used to be a wreck when we were children, but Luc put it together again plank by plank. There's no one else there, just Luc. It's the place he goes to when he wants to be alone.'

'So…this flight to the ranch?' Emma asked casually.

'No,' Karina said flatly. 'I've changed my mind. Luc would never forgive me if he thought I'd let you go to the ranch on your own. We won't even contemplate his reaction if you turned up at the cabin—'

'And I won't forgive you if you don't tell me how to get there,' Emma threatened. 'Please…' She grabbed Karina's hand.

Seeing she was set on going, Karina relented. 'The Carrier Pigeon would take you as far as the ranch—'

'The Carrier Pigeon?'

'That's what we call the Marcelos light aircraft

that shuttles back and forth between the city and the ranch. You'd be safe at the ranch, but you can't get to the cabin because you would need to ride there—there's no other way. There are no roads or landing strips. And you don't ride, *do* you, Emma?' Karina demanded in her best attempt at a stern voice.

Emma's shoulders lifted in a reluctant shrug. 'If I could just get to the ranch…'

'Anyway, Luc doesn't pick up calls when he's at the cabin, so you'll have to wait for him at the ranch. And goodness knows how long he plans to stay at the cabin. It's in a really remote area. The only way Luc can be contacted is by satellite phone, and then he never picks up.'

'I'm happy to wait at the ranch,' Emma said blandly.

Karina studied her face. 'You wouldn't try anything stupid, would you?'

'Of course not,' Emma protested, eyes open wide. 'I'd really like to visit the ranch…if I wouldn't get in the way?'

'You wouldn't get in the way,' Karina confirmed, glancing up.

'Well, then. Will you fix it for me?' Emma held her breath.

'I could ring to let the staff at the ranch know that you're coming, but that doesn't mean they'll be able to get hold of Luc. He switches off completely at the cabin. That's why he goes there. You'd be on your own until he got back.'

'That's fine by me. I wouldn't mind, if I'm not going to be too much trouble for the staff?'

What did she have to lose? She had to see Luc. And as things stood, she was on her own anyway.

CHAPTER FOURTEEN

HORSE-RIDING CAME with a far better press than it deserved, Emma thought as she stared down a stable block that boasted snorting firebrands in every stall. Did people actually enjoy sitting on top of a volcano? She'd only arrived at Luc's ranch that lunchtime and, after being collected at the landing strip by an elderly gaucho who had introduced himself as Pedro, she had quickly settled in and then come straight here.

Her first sight of Pedro had thrilled her, and not just because seeing him had told her she was closer to Luc. With his outfit of battered leather chaps, coin belt and typical hat, garnished with old-world manners, the elderly gaucho had made her feel special from the moment she'd arrived. It was Pedro she was trying to convince now—

and not that well—that she had to borrow one of these horses.

'I've been riding since I could walk,' she asserted airily, hoping he couldn't see her shaking.

He sized her up. 'I'll fetch you a mount.'

'Thank you.' She smiled. Job done.

He brought out a mule.

'I'm to ride that?' she said, trying not to be unkind as she looked into the doleful eyes of the clearly ancient animal.

'*Sim, senhorita.* Nancy is slow, but she is kind. You will be safe.'

Hmm. Biting back her apprehension, she approached the apparently docile animal and stroked her long, velvety ears. Nancy was cute, but that was her assessment while her feet were firmly planted on the ground.

'She is grandmother here,' Pedro explained, his weather-beaten face creasing in a smile.

'Oh, good.' Perhaps Nancy and she would get along after all. She had always had an affinity with older people.

'And Nancy knows the way to the cabin.'

'The cabin?' Emma adopted an innocent expression. She had intended to go it alone, but any information she could garner from Pedro was all to the good.

'*Sim.*' Pedro was busily checking all the straps and buckles required before she could mount up. She didn't want to get Pedro into trouble. 'Wouldn't Senhor Marcelos be angry if I interrupted his solitude?' she asked carefully.

'Senhor Marcelos is never angry with Pedro. I will accompany you.'

'Oh, no—that's not necessary.' She quickly turned away as her cheeks burned red. She had no idea what everyone thought of her sudden arrival at the ranch house, and could only presume that Karina had called them and made some excuse or other—saying that she worked for their boss, perhaps. 'I've got a phone for security.' She brandished it to make the point that she was really together and ready for this.

'That won't work here,' Pedro said flatly, reaching beneath his hat to scratch his head.

'And I've got supplies from the kitchen.' The

saddlebags she was carrying were bulging with food and water. Pedro couldn't argue with that. And then there was her trump card. 'And I've got a map.' She produced it triumphantly.

Pedro shook his head. He didn't seem happy at all, but as he said nothing more about it she felt confident that he was going to let her ride out on her own now that she had proved to be so organised.

'You like it here?' Pedro asked, smiling up at her as he tightened the strap beneath the mule's stomach.

'It's fabulous,' Emma said honestly. So fabulous it was hard to take in everything Pedro had shown her.

He'd had driven her for miles from the landing strip, across Luc's land, he told her, until they came to a towering archway that marked the boundary of the main house. It had taken them another twenty minutes before the sprawling ranch house had come into view. Things were on such a vast scale she could easily see why Luc belonged here. He was a big man from a land whose scale she was still getting used to. The stark beauty of the pampas had struck her in the heart as she'd flown over it. Perhaps because it was wild and seemingly unknowable, like him.

The kindness shown to her by Luc's staff had told her a lot about him. They couldn't do enough for her—even when she said she was going out on a ride just a few short hours after arriving. Excitement at the thought of seeing Luc again didn't allow for delay. Not even her glorious guest room, with its billowing white canopy over the huge four-poster bed, could tempt her to stay.

Now, if she could just get her leg over the saddle...

She was supposed to be an experienced rider, remember that?

Thankfully, Pedro cupped his hands and gave her a leg up, but even on the back of a mule it felt a long way down to the ground. No handrails?

No handrails.

He was splitting logs when Pedro called him.

'What?' He ran to his horse while Pedro was

still explaining that he was trailing Emma at a distance.

'I won't let any harm come to her,' his old friend assured him.

Not good enough. Luc had to see Emma for himself. He had to know she was safe. Out here on the pampas there were miles of apparent nothingness, and if a stranger wasn't wary they could easily get lost. Emma might panic. The mule could trip. There were countless risks for the unwary traveller. He wasn't about to take any chances where Emma's safety was concerned. Stowing the phone, he sprang onto his stallion's back without wasting time saddling up. His first aim was to make her safe. The second was to come clean. Karina was right in that it had done him good, coming out here away from every distraction. It had shown him what counted and what didn't. His pride was nowhere on that list. Emma's peace of mind was the headline event.

As he urged his mount across land he knew intimately, he felt strong and certain. When he told Emma the truth he would be anything but.

He wasn't used to making himself vulnerable. As a youth he'd been so sure-footed and confident—until he'd got the biggest slap in the face of his life. At the time he'd been stunned. Then he'd been driven by bitterness and revenge. It had turned him cold until Emma had shown him a different way. Talking it through with her would either end things between them for good, or prove that people could change, and that he was trying.

As much as he liked to be in control, this was one occasion when Emma would be his judge and jury, and he wouldn't be able to control or influence the outcome.

His first impulse when he spotted her was to laugh—with sheer relief, and with happiness and amusement at the sight of a very determined woman trying to coax a mule up a hill. Leaning almost flat on Nancy's neck as the old mule took every opportunity to snatch mouthfuls of her favourite herbs, Emma was holding a carrot in front of Nancy's muzzle. It wasn't getting her very far. Nancy was too clever to be fooled, and

was as stubborn as a mule was supposed to be.
Nancy had her head in the air and was content-
edly munching, with long strands of grass escap-
ing from either side of her mouth. This forced
Emma to hold the carrot higher and higher, with
the end result that neither of them was going anywhere fast.

'Luc!'

Emma sat up so abruptly when she saw him
he was frightened she would spook the mule.
He brought his horse to a skidding halt across
Nancy's bows, and scooping Emma up, he de-
posited her on the stallion in front of him.

'Luc!' she exclaimed, turning to face him.
'What a surprise to see you.'

'Yeah,' he said drily. 'Imagine that. What are
the chances?'

'I'm glad I found you.' She smiled as if she really meant it.

'Glad I found *you*, don't you mean?' he said,
urging his stallion forward. 'You are an extremely
reckless woman.'

'In Scotland you criticised me for not being adventurous enough,' she argued, bouncing stiffly in front of him.

'I didn't expect you to take your adventuring to these lengths.' Putting an arm around her waist, he drew her close. 'Lean into me—move with me. We have to move as one.'

'I'm not sure I—'

'I know you can. That's one thing I do know for sure.'

'Maybe I could relax if there was something to hang on to.'

'I won't let you fall.' He brought his mouth close to her ear to say this. The temptation to taste her neck was overwhelming.

'How will you steer if you're hanging on to me?' Her voice was tight with tension.

'How I always do...with my thighs.'

She stiffened and held herself away from him, but not before he'd felt the shiver of arousal that coursed through her frame. 'Take hold of some mane and hang on to that, if it makes you feel safer,' he suggested.

'I'm perfectly relaxed,' she assured him through

gritted teeth. 'But, what about the mule? We can't just leave her here.'

'Pedro will take her home.'

'Pedro?' She sounded shocked as she glanced around. 'Has Pedro followed me all this way?'

'Did you seriously think he would allow you to ride out here on your own? You told him you didn't want company, apparently, but thankfully he had more sense than to set you loose on thousands of acres of pampas.'

'He needn't have worried,' she said, frowning as she shook her head. 'I brought a map.'

'That makes all the difference,' he agreed drily.

'Are you being sarcastic?'

'Would I?' A subtle twitch of his thighs was all it took to urge his stallion forward from a loping walk to a bouncing trot.

'You did that on purpose,' Emma accused him through chattering teeth.

He smiled as he held her close, relishing the sensation of having Emma in his arms again. He urged his horse into a smooth, rolling canter, and from being as stiff as a board, Emma was gradually learning to relax. 'You mustn't ride out here on your own.'

'Why not?'

'Because there are dangerous animals—'

'None more dangerous that you,' she said.

He laughed as he took his stallion forward from a canter to a gallop, wondering when he'd ever felt so free as he headed with single-minded purpose towards the cabin.

Did Luc have to be quite so provocative? *Or quite so sexy?* She wasn't here to go to bed with him but to get things sorted out once and for all. Then, if it was over between them, her heart would break, but she'd have to get over it for the sake of their child.

Luc had slowed his stallion to an ambling walk as they approached the stretch leading to the cabin.

'I kept my promise,' he said. 'I didn't let you fall.'

'It must have been tempting,' she suggested, testing him.

He didn't play. This wasn't Lucas Marcelos, the smooth businessman from the city with his private jet. This was a man who battled nature, not a man who battled spreadsheets on a desk. And this version of Luc looked way beyond sexy with his sharp black stubble, swarthy skin and his wild, unruly hair. She loved the way he rode bareback in battered jeans and boots and just an old shirt with the sleeves rolled up. She loved everything about him…

She loved him.

'Daydreaming again?'

'Just enjoying the ride,' she said quickly.

'Now I know you're lying.'

'No. Seriously. I'm not.'

Could there be anything more romantic than riding on a stallion with this man across this land? The rhythm of the horse's hooves, together with the undulation of the horse's body was the best workout she'd ever had. And it was soothing. She almost wished that she belonged here too.

She pressed back against Luc's chest, relishing his strength and his heat. He was so virile, so potent, and here, in this wild country, she was glad of his command. There was nothing soft or easy about the pampas. Like the man riding behind her, it was hard and challenging, but full of opportunity too—or was that her imagination running riot again?

'I'll teach you how to ride one day.'

One day. The phrase remained in her head like a charm, a talisman. Could they really make it work *one day*?

Luc reined in outside the cabin. Nestled in the lee of a hill, it looked so welcoming. 'Will you really teach me how to ride?' she asked impulsively.

When Luc didn't answer right away, she took that as a no. She probably wouldn't be here long enough, Emma reasoned.

But while she was here, she would live and love and take her chances. That was how Luc's wild land made her feel.

He sprang down first, and turning to her, he lifted her into his arms. Backing his way through the door, he lowered her onto her feet on a lovingly polished wooden floor. The whole place smelled of beeswax and coffee. Steadying her, he stepped back, but she wasn't in the mood for half measures. Putting her arms around his neck she hugged him tight. It was too late to worry about what he thought. The way she felt about him had to find expression.

'What was that for?'

Angling her chin, she stared up at him.

'Why aren't you saying anything?' The corner of Luc's mouth lifted in a smile. 'What do you want me to do?'

'Kiss me?'

Barely a heartbeat passed before he dragged her into his arms.

CHAPTER FIFTEEN

SHE WAS INSTANTLY LOST. Drunk on Luc's consuming power, his strength, his familiar scent, his touch, the taste of him and, most of all, the way her heart sang when they were close. Her body ached to be one with his. There was no other man who could do that to her. He was the one, the only one. He completed her. He made her strong. But if Luc couldn't open up and talk about the past, and his plan for the future, her visit here was a waste of time.

He pulled back to look at her. 'What's this?' He caught a tear on the pad of his thumb.

'Pain,' she admitted, gritting her teeth.

'Pain?' Luc demanded, anxious at once. 'Not the baby?'

'Riding?' She grimaced as she admitted this.

'My bottom is in agony. Why on earth do people do it?'

Luc laughed softly. 'Maybe I'll show you someday.' He rested his brow against hers and they shared a smile. Somehow the mundane applied to the soaring tensions they both had to face made a bridge between them. 'You want to talk?' he prompted.

'Yes. About you,' she said. 'If we don't, I'll go back to Scotland.'

He led her over to the old battered sofa in front of the fire and invited her to sit. He brought coffee for them both from the pot on the stove, and set it on the table in front of them. 'Invisible housekeeper,' he explained.

She smiled ruefully, knowing that whatever they said about Luc liking his solitude, he liked his home comforts too, and that there would be someone, not too far away, who would make sure that he had everything he needed.

'Pedro's wife,' he explained, putting her mind at rest.

Leaning back against the wall, Luc stared at

her with a thoughtful expression on his face. 'I need to get some things off my chest.'

'I know,' she said quietly.

'I've been married before.'

She didn't know that, and couldn't have been more shocked. The silence lengthened, and she was glad she was sitting down. This was the last thing she had expected. Her heart seemed to have stopped beating. Her throat had dried. In spite of the blazing fire she felt chilled and uncertain. Everything she had built her belief on when it came to Luc had turned out to be wrong. Lucas Marcelos, the man she thought she knew, was just a construct of her over-fertile imagination. 'Married.' Now she said the word, she didn't know why the possibility of Luc being married at one time hadn't occurred to her before.

'My wife is dead.'

For the second time in as many minutes, she felt the world tilt on its axis. 'How?'

'She was killed with her lover in a freak accident,' Luc explained in a voice that held no emotion.

Her lover? Luc's wife had had a lover? That seemed incredible—unbelievable, to Emma.

'I was very young,' he explained. 'She was too. We moved with the same fast set. I should have kept my baby sister away from them. That's what crucifies me. Karina was just a little girl, wrapped up in the glamour of an aunt who was beautiful and exciting, and whose lover was careless and daring. The accident that killed my wife and my lover almost killed my sister too. He was showing off and ran his car off the road with my wife and Karina in it. Karina escaped with just cuts and bruises, but my wife and her lover were killed outright.'

The bitterness in Luc's voice didn't surprise her, and when he stopped telling her the story she could imagine him running it scene by scene in front of his eyes, and the true facts would only be embellished by his imagination. When the police had told her about her parents' accident, it hadn't been what they or the emergency services had told her, but what she'd pictured in her mind that still haunted her.

'I will never forgive myself for exposing my sister to danger likc that.'

'But it wasn't your fault, Luc.'

'It was my fault,' he insisted, pulling away from the wall. 'I didn't have to be at the scene of the accident for it to be my fault. I pushed my wife into the arms of her lover. If I had spent more time with her, instead of playing polo and building a business, she might not have taken a lover in the first place, but I was full of the arrogance of youth, and I neglected her. She was young and beautiful, and she wanted a life. She didn't want to be sitting at home, waiting for me to come back. And why should she? I was in the wrong, Emma. I treated my wife like just another possession—as I treated you when we first met.'

'But at some point you have to forgive yourself, Luc.'

'As you have forgiven yourself for your parents' deaths?'

She couldn't answer that without admitting that she was always looking for something she'd missed—something that could have saved them long before they'd gone on that drug-fuelled journey to disaster.

'Guilt isn't easy to shift. I just don't want to do that to anyone else, and I almost did…with you. And with you it's worse.' Luc's gaze steadied on her face. 'I thought I loved my wife, and I felt betrayed when she took a lover, but now I know that I didn't love her, and that what I felt was an adolescent emotion so very different from what I feel for you.'

'I'm sorry for her death,' Emma said quietly, reeling as she tried to take in what Luc had just said.

The silence that followed was absolute.

'We can't decide the path that others take,' Luc said at last, 'But actions have consequences, as I have proved yet again. And I'm frightened, of losing you, frightened of making the same mistake again. I've never been frightened like this in my life before.' His eyes searched out her gaze.

Standing, she took hold of his hands and held them firmly in hers. 'Love is terrifying. You feel so much, and then there's this point where you're

270 BRAZILIAN'S NINE MONTHS' NOTICE

totally committed to that one person, but you're not sure that they feel the same. That's frightening. That's walking a tightrope without a safety net. But you have to take that risk or you'll never know.' She paused for breath. 'I love you with all my heart. There. I've said it. I can't help myself. I can't stop myself—'

'*Agradeço a Deus por você!*'

Luc's voice was muffled in her shoulder. Winding her fingers through his hair, she held him close, and for a few moments they stood together, breathing in harmony as they accepted that maybe they didn't have to go on alone from here.

'Translate,' she whispered.

Lifting his head, Luc stared into her eyes. 'Thank God for you, Emma.'

His heart welled with love for Emma, and for the stand she was taking. He loved her for her resilience, whatever life threw at her. This was the woman he wanted at his side. This was the woman who would fight for his children and protect them to her last breath. He had wasted too much time indulging in thoughts of revenge, when there was no revenge possible as the protagonists were dead. Was he going to allow the past to colour every decision he made? Wasn't it time to move forward, instead of looking back?

'What are you doing now?' Emma demanded as he knelt at her feet.

'I'm humbly asking you to be my wife.'

'Humbly?' she said, raising a brow.

'As humbly as I can.'

A smile lit up her face. 'Not humbly at all, then.' She was silent for a while as they stared at each other, and then she frowned and said, 'You're serious, aren't you?'

'Never more so,' he admitted.

Pressing her lips together, she smiled and shook her head. 'Do you have to look like such a bad boy when you say such lovely things?'

He tipped his chin as he admitted ruefully, 'Apparently so.'

'In that case…'

Kneeling in front of him, Emma reached out and he took her hands in his.

'I'm even more frightened now,' she admitted.

'You, frightened?'

'Well…' Her slanting smile lit up her eyes. 'Perhaps a little apprehensive of what I'm taking on.'

'Not half as apprehensive as I am,' he admitted drily.

'Love has been an alien and scary concept to me too,' she admitted, 'and for so long. My weird, dysfunctional past has left me wary like you, but I know that what I feel for you, and what I feel for our child is one of life's gloriously unavoidable emotions, and it's taken hold of me and will never let me go. It heals, it hurts, it thrills. It's love. And I am a hostage for life.'

'So that's a yes?'

'I think I've kept you on your knees long enough,' she teased. 'Yes. That's the happiest yes you'll ever hear.'

Bringing Emma into his arms, he kissed her, then raising her to her feet, he backed her towards the bedroom. 'Food can wait,' he said, nuzzling his lips against her neck. 'You're not going to faint with hunger, are you?'

'Only with pleasure,' she said, her eyes laughing into his.

She was shivering with need as Luc moved over her. She quickly helped him to take off her clothes. Sensation was everything. Heat was firing along every nerve ending she possessed. She was desperate to feel him naked, skin to skin. She seized hold of his shirt, dealing with the buttons frantically and then sliding it from his shoulders. Her hunger mounted as she felt his muscles ripple and bunch beneath her hands. Grabbing the buckle on his belt, she loosened his trousers. She felt for him and he sprang free. She clasped him, laughing softly at the fact that her hand would barely encompass him. 'I want to taste you,' she said.

'Be my guest.' Removing his jeans, Luc tossed them away. Rolling onto his back he meshed his fingers through her hair as she moved down the bed and took him. Suckling and lapping, for the sheer pleasure of hearing him groan, she stroked his powerful chest as she pleasured him, her own arousal mounting as she anticipated the moment when the tables would be turned. She didn't have long to wait. Luc was impatient to have her. They were both greedy.

She laughed with excitement as he brought her beneath him. Lifting her so her head was on the pillows, he moved slowly down the bed. Taking hold of her wrists, he held them above her head. Closing her eyes as he kissed his way around her body, she smiled as sensation flooded her, and her heart throbbed with love.

'I should have remembered how greedy you were,' Luc said, his voice tight with lust as she raised her hips, demanding more contact. Resting her legs over the wide spread of his shoulders, so that she was completely exposed, completely vulnerable, he kissed her. Luc was a master of seduction, an expert at temptation, and he knew exactly which buttons to press. 'No,' he warned softly. 'Not yet.'

He made her wait, which made her hungrier

still for him, and it seemed for ever before he eased back, and then very slowly moved forward again. Taking her, he stretched her and filled her as he claimed her. He was so careful with her, so controlled. She trusted him completely, and the feeling had never been more extreme as he took her deeply. Pausing a moment to allow her to grow used to the sensation, he only had to roll his hips to make it impossible for her to hold on. Crying out wildly and repeatedly, she ceded control of everything gladly, to pleasure and to oneness with Luc.

'More?' he suggested with amusement when, after the longest time, she finally grew quiet.

Her answer was a look as she bore down firmly, taking him.

Luc answered this by pinning her hands above her head. He loomed over her, and then he took her fast and hard. Her world exploded. His did too.

She wasn't sure how long exactly they stayed in bed. The time they spent together couldn't be measured in hours, only in pleasure, and that was extreme. She went for water in the kitchen and when he found her there, they made love again. Luc lifted her onto the counter and nudged his way between her thighs. Then he carried her back to bed and made love to her again. His stamina was inexhaustible, and when she woke the sun was streaming strongly into the room and Luc was working some magic with his hands.

'Your needs match mine,' he whispered as she stared at him sleepily.

'What a great way to wake up.'

Eventually they fell asleep again, entwined in each other's arms, and when she woke dusk had fallen, and Luc was behind her, one hand pressing her down so he could watch as he pleasured her. 'Maybe this is the best way to wake up,' she gasped into the pillow, crying out as he tipped her over the edge. Reaching back, she moved fiercely with him, gripping his buttocks with fingers like iron, working him mercilessly until Luc fell too. They slept some more and then they bathed together. She sat between his legs in the tub, resting back against his chest as Luc kissed her neck and lazily soaped her.

'You're so relaxed after sex,' he commented, nuzzling her hair back so he could expose her sensitive skin.

'I'm exhausted,' she admitted, smiling.

'At last.' He laughed.

Leaving the water, he pulled a towel down from the heated rail and held it out for her. She was practically purring as he cocooned her in its fluffy warmth. Resting her head against his shoulder, she smiled as he wrapped his arms around her. There was nothing else on earth like this. Just being with Luc was enough.

She'd left his ranch in such a rush she hadn't thought to bring any spare clothes with her. She borrowed his shirt—a shirt for a giant. She wore it like a dress. Her feet were bare and her hair was gathered back in a ponytail. There was no artifice between them, no tension, no pride. They made a meal together in the kitchen, laughing as they shared the tasks. It seemed like the most natural thing on earth to her. She had never been more relaxed.

'So, soon-to-be Senhora Marcelos,' Luc murmured, standing behind her so he could wrap his arms around her waist. 'When you live with me and be my love, and we have a football team of children, will you still find time to work and help me build up my business?'

'Don't worry about my commitment to my work. I will be energised. I have every intention of adding a human touch to your increasingly efficient machine.'

'And you'll still find time to make love with me?'

'If we're going to have a team of children, I think I'll have to,' she pointed out pragmatically.

'I'll have it written into your contract, just to be sure,' Luc said, acting stern. 'Along with my promise to love and cherish you, even when I teach you to ride—'

'Oh, that,' she said.

'Yes, that.'

'I've been meaning to talk to you about those riding lessons.' She grimaced.

Luc held out his hand to her with a wicked smile on his face that she recognised at once. 'Come,' he coaxed. 'I'll teach you the basics in the bedroom.'

'In that case...'

Suddenly riding didn't seem like such a bad idea.

EPILOGUE

'NOW WE JUST have to find a man worthy of my new sister,' Emma insisted as Karina cradled the two new additions to the Marcelos family in her arms. They were all staying on the ranch for a while to give Emma a chance to settle into her new role as the mother of twins, while Karina, who was staying in one of the guest cottages, had the opportunity to get to know her baby niece and nephew.

'A man for me?' Karina huffed. 'Not interested. I've had enough of men to last me a lifetime. Sorry,' she added, not sounding sorry at all as she handed over one of Emma's twins. 'I do realise you've got to put up with Lucas, and though I'd love to be a sister-in-arms at this stressful time for you, I prefer my freedom. Can't even pretend for your sake that I'm in any hurry to bring another rampaging barbarian into my life.'

'Lucas hasn't left your life. He never will.'

'I believe you—unfortunately.' Karina laughed. 'So, what are you cooking up for me on the man front?' she demanded with a suspicious look.

'Nothing,' Emma protested, not very convincingly. 'Luc's bringing some friends over for supper, that's all. Why don't you stay? You don't have to dash back to the guest cottage right away, do you?'

Karina raised a brow. 'Stay and play dangerous games with bad boys? No, thank you. You're already drowning in hormones so the testosterone overload will barely touch you, but I'm vulnerable to attack.'

Emma laughed. 'I don't think any man could get the better of you, Karina Marcelos. What?' she pressed when Karina fell silent.

'It has been known,' Karina admitted. 'When I was young and foolish.'

'You fell for someone?' Emma pressed.

'Just no polo players, okay?'

Knowing when to leave things alone, Emma changed the subject. Putting the twins down in their respective cots, she went to join Karina at the window and they chatted until the door swung open and a group of men arrived in arrow formation, headed up by Luc. He walked straight to Emma and, oblivious to the fact that there were other people in the room, he drew her into his arms and kissed her as if they were alone. 'I love you,' he whispered. 'I've been away for far too long.'

'You've been away on this ranch within half a mile of here for half a day's polo training,' Emma pointed out as Luc nuzzled his stubble against her neck, making her shiver with desire for him.

'Half a day is too long,' Luc growled ominously. 'I brought the team home to see the twins. I hope you don't mind.'

'No, of course not.' Emma turned to Karina, only to confront her ashen-faced and on the point of leaving. 'Is something wrong? Won't you stay?' she said discreetly.

'No, thank you.' Karina gave her a warm hug. 'I haven't changed my mind. I'll see you tomorrow.'

'Why are you in such a rush? Just give them a chance,' Emma said, glancing at the group of good-looking polo players—big, tough men, currently cooing over the next generation of the Marcelos dynasty.

'Because I already gave them a chance,' Karina said in a forced whisper.

'All of them?' Emma queried, opening her eyes.

'One of them,' Karina said with a meaningful look. 'And I don't need another rampaging barbarian in my life. I'm going to leave you to it—okay?'

Karina had almost made it out of the door when Luc put out a hand, stopping her. 'You know Dante Baracca, don't you, Karina? And this is my wife, Emma. May I present the latest recruit to Team Thunderbolt?'

Something told Emma that Dante Baracca was no stranger to Karina. He certainly wasn't interested in anyone else in the room, though Karina seemed tense and angry as she nodded her head in acknowledgement that she already knew the dark stranger. It couldn't be just the look of him, Emma reasoned. With a brother like hers, Karina had grown up with men like Dante. The entire Thunderbolt team conformed to the same dark and swarthy, hard-muscled type. Extending her hand in greeting, she weighed up the new arrival. 'Pleased to meet you, Senhor Baracca.'

'And you, *senhora*.' Dante Baracca bowed over her hand, but his heat was reserved for Karina. There wasn't so much a crackle of electricity between them as a lightning strike, Emma thought, looking on with interest as they eyed each other up like a matador with a bull. What was the matter with them both? Why had this suddenly become a scowling contest? 'Do you two know each other?' she asked Karina, tongue in cheek as they walked together to the door.

'You could say that,' Karina admitted reluctantly.

'So you know Dante from some time back?' Emma pressed gently, concerned for her sister-in-law. 'He didn't do anything he shouldn't, did he?'

'I try to avoid him,' was as much as Karina was

prepared to say as she directed a stinging look at the man in question.

'Surely, he's not all bad?'

Karina narrowed her eyes, and before Emma had chance to ask her friend any more questions Luc had returned to claim her.

'I'm shooing them away now,' he said, bringing his face close to growl this against her neck. 'If you think I'm going to wait any longer to hold you in my arms, you're seriously mistaken. The babies are asleep and I want you now.'

'You're impatient,' Emma whispered, trying not to smile with pleasure at her husband's eagerness to bed her.

'Do you blame me?'

'No. I love a man who's firm and decisive.'

'Firm you can count on. Decisive? Certainly. So, if you want more of my direction—'

'In the bedroom only,' she warned.

Luc shrugged. 'I'll settle for that for now, though anything else is up for grabs.'

'Anything else is up for debate after I follow your direction in the bedroom,' Emma teased. 'And since you've been away such a very long time, I've been able to think up a few ideas of my own.'

'I leave you alone for a couple of hours and see what happens?' Luc exhaled a mock-weary sigh. 'Shall we?' he suggested, pointing to the door.

'I think we should,' Emma agreed as the nannies took care of the babies, and the housekeeper came to escort their guests away to the dining room where a spread had been laid out for them. But before they made it to the bedroom there was one question on her mind: 'Who *is* Dante Baracca?'

'That's a question for another day,' Luc informed her. Closing the door so they were alone at last, he turned to face his wife. 'Right now I've only got one thing on my mind, and that is making love to my wife until she falls asleep exhausted in my arms.'

'That's become quite a habit around here,' Emma observed, smiling.

'And one I intend to maintain,' Luc assured her as he backed her towards the bed.

* * * * *

MILLS & BOON®
Large Print – March 2016

A Christmas Vow of Seduction
Maisey Yates

Brazilian's Nine Months' Notice
Susan Stephens

The Sheikh's Christmas Conquest
Sharon Kendrick

Shackled to the Sheikh
Trish Morey

Unwrapping the Castelli Secret
Caitlin Crews

A Marriage Fit for a Sinner
Maya Blake

Larenzo's Christmas Baby
Kate Hewitt

His Lost-and-Found Bride
Scarlet Wilson

Housekeeper Under the Mistletoe
Cara Colter

Gift-Wrapped in Her Wedding Dress
Kandy Shepherd

The Prince's Christmas Vow
Jennifer Faye

MILLS & BOON®
Large Print – April 2016

The Price of His Redemption
Carol Marinelli

Back in the Brazilian's Bed
Susan Stephens

The Innocent's Sinful Craving
Sara Craven

Brunetti's Secret Son
Maya Blake

Talos Claims His Virgin
Michelle Smart

Destined for the Desert King
Kate Walker

Ravensdale's Defiant Captive
Melanie Milburne

The Best Man & The Wedding Planner
Teresa Carpenter

Proposal at the Winter Ball
Jessica Gilmore

Bodyguard...to Bridegroom?
Nikki Logan

Christmas Kisses with Her Boss
Nina Milne

0316 Rom LP